WHERE GOD BEGAN

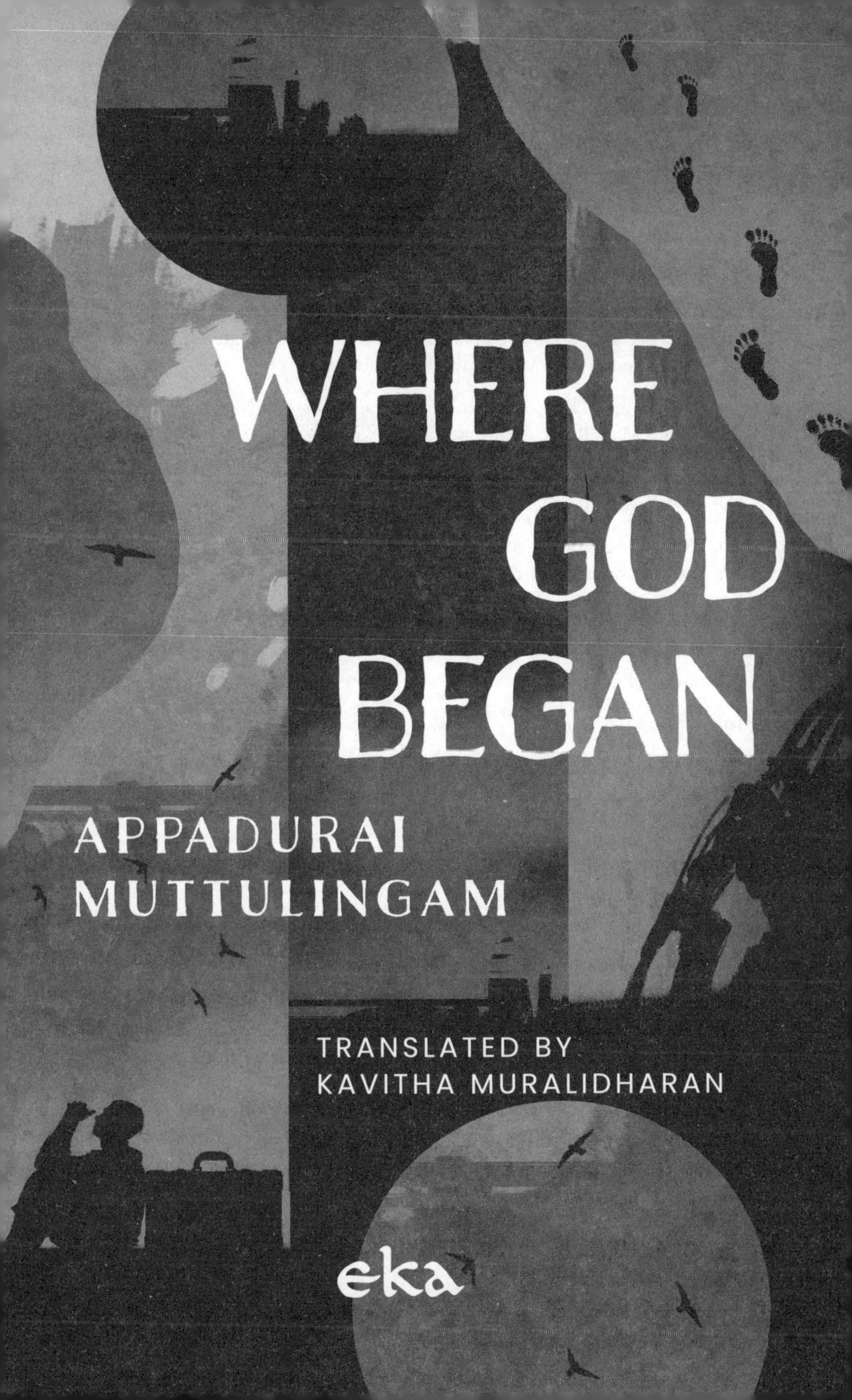
WHERE GOD BEGAN
APPADURAI MUTTULINGAM
TRANSLATED BY
KAVITHA MURALIDHARAN
eka

eka

First published in Tamil as *Kadavul Thodangiya Idam* in 2014 by Vikatan Publications

Published in English as *Where God Began* in 2023 by Eka, an imprint of Westland Books, a division of Nasadiya Technologies Private Limited, by arrangement with Kalachuvadu Publications

No. 269/2B, First Floor, 'Irai Arul', Vimalraj Street, Nethaji Nagar, Alapakkam Main Road, Maduravoyal, Chennai 600095

ISBN: 9789357769013

10 9 8 7 6 5 4 3 2 1

This is a work of fiction. Names, characters, organisations, places, events and incidents are either products of the author's imagination or used fictitiously.

Typeset by Jojy Philip, New Delhi

Printed at Parksons Graphics Pvt. Ltd

Contents

ONE

Leaving

They had a meeting at home to decide what to do with me. My Appa, Amma, uncle and grandmother were all in attendance. Even my younger sister was present. Yet I had been kept in the dark and I was furious. The culprit: my sister. A boy from the freedom movement, who studied with me, was a frequent visitor to our house, raising my sister's suspicion that I would soon join 'the movement'—which led to this emergency meeting. Amma promptly sold her land to arrange funds for the agent to make travel plans to evacuate me. Appa spoke to a relative of an uncle in Germany. He had apparently given some assurances and things were moving rapidly.

'You can't stay in Jaffna a moment longer, Nishant. You'll be sent to stay with your uncle in Colombo. This will help the agent coordinate with you after the departure dates are finalised,' I was told and packed off to Colombo.

Since the agent said it would take about six months, and in order not to waste time and to make some pocket money, I joined a restaurant upon reaching Colombo. My job was to maintain accounts. Besides keeping a record of expenses and income on a daily basis, I was also expected to write letters in English. Most of the correspondence was addressed to government offices. The letters would typically begin with 'Most respected Sir' and end with 'Obediently yours'.

As if these were not enough, the cashier to whom I had taken an instant dislike, would stand outside the room and enquire repeatedly if my work was done. Perhaps the feeling was mutual. My friend said that the owner of the shop was called Jumper. It was difficult to make out if the name was that of a Tamil or a Sinhalese. The owner was equally fluent in Tamil, Sinhalese and English, making it difficult to hazard a guess. 'He has several cases against him, but he always manages to jump over them,' one of my friends working there had said, by way of explaining the unusual name. The owner would often travel abroad and visit the restaurant only once or twice a month. The cashier acted as the manager, taking care of everything.

The first two weeks were somewhat uneventful. On the sixteenth day, a six-footer with a broad face and a broader moustache arrived. Nudging me, my friend said, 'Jumper, Jumper.' He was wearing a yellow shirt and a sarong with a broad black belt holding it in place. Small-time rowdies in Colombo tied the sarong in front, over the belly. The formidable ones walked around with the sarong tucked in firmly at the back. Jumper looked intimidating. The cashier was having a word with him. Later, he pointed to me and said something. Just as I thought it was all over, the cashier snapped his fingers, calling me over.

Jumper looked at me like I was an object he intended to buy. 'Are you Nishant the dickhead?' he asked.

'My first name is Nishant. The other one could probably be what you just gave me,' I said, unperturbed.

Jumper's face betrayed no change. 'I don't have time for a murder today. I'm occupied with something more serious. I'll deal with you some other time. You may leave now,' he said. I returned home with a salary for the three weeks I had worked there.

One day, I received a telephone call asking to prepare for the journey abroad. Appa, Amma and my sister came over to Colombo to send me off. Appa gave me a suitcase he had used before he was married. It smelt of Appa when I opened it. I bought two thick sweaters thinking that they would do for a Russian winter. My uncle bought me a second-hand overcoat from the Pettah market. It looked exactly like an old overcoat from an old market. It had probably been used by a bodybuilder, because it flopped hopelessly over my shoulders and back and could accommodate another person when I put it on. Wearing the coat, I looked transformed—like the beggar in the movie *Dr Zhivago*. I looked at my sister, who was trying hard to suppress her laughter.

Uncle had a hefty dog, which would jump and lick me as if he was my pet. I had not lifted a finger for the dog, but, on seeing me return home from anywhere, this dog named Musa would bound towards me excitedly and then roll on his back. He would then get to its feet, trembling and, in its frenzy, often leak a drop of piss too. I had no idea what to do with a dog that loved me so much.

As I stood before the mirror, admiring the overcoat, Musa bit me on the calf. Amma was instantly worried and, viewing it as a bad omen, demanded that I postpone my journey. Uncle took me to a doctor who gave me an injection and advised me not to worry since it was a pet dog.

The agent treated the incident as if it was of no consequence and asked me to be at the airport on time. He was planning to send eight people on that day. He would come to the airport but not travel with my group. Also, only he knew who the other seven travellers were. The eight people about to travel together that day were strangers to one another, and it had been made clear that they should not attempt to find each other before reaching Russia. They would be introduced in Russia. The agent said that I would have to leave on 3 August 1992 on a Russian Aeroflot, which would reach Moscow via Pakistan. A student visa for Moscow had been organised for me.

The immigration officer at Colombo had only one question, for which I wasn't prepared. The agent hadn't trained me for that. 'What will you study in Russia?' he had asked. I had no such intention. I wanted to reach Germany, crossing the Russian border. I said 'architecture'—the first thing that popped into my mind. The white-collared officer believed me. He raised the stamp chest-high and stamped my passport with a thump. When he handed the passport back to me, I thought, this would be the first and the last stamp on my Sri Lankan passport.

Seated in the waiting lounge, I looked around and began the game of guessing who the other seven people bound for Russia were. One or two could be identified easily. Most of the travellers seated there spoke Sinhala. Some would get off in Karachi. There were very few women. Everybody looked like they were on a business trip. A young man struggling to be inconspicuous buried himself in a chair as if it were a bunker. He could be nineteen or twenty years of age. He might be one of the group. There was a middle-aged Tamil with two bags who wore no cardigan or coat. He could be another of them. There was another man, of about thirty-five. He looked educated and was probably a teacher. I wondered if I could smile at him. The man looked charismatic.

Then, a woman walked in, making a clacking sound. All eyes followed her, like they were watching a tennis match. She was wearing jeans and a T-shirt—no sweater. She looked like an educated Tamil girl, barely twenty. She was holding a Sri Lankan passport and some documents. She wasn't carrying a handbag, but a big beautiful black bag hung from her shoulder. She walked as if she were balancing a crown. When crossing the doorway, she made her way warily, carrying her bag carefully. Then she walked towards a seat far from mine, as if that spot had been reserved for her, and sat down and crossed her legs.

Passengers continued to trickle in. It was well past departure time, yet there was no announcement. Suddenly there was one, as if someone had realised the mistake. The flight would be delayed by an hour. Soon enough, there was another announcement. Calling out a name, the announcer insisted that the person approach the reception desk. Nobody responded. Two officers walked swiftly towards the girl and spoke to her. They then dragged her. Her outsized black bag got left behind on the chair. Her cries 'I am not the one, I am not the one' reverberated across the waiting lounge for a long time. Long after the drama ended, the haunting words still hung in the air: I am not the one.

The incident left several passengers unnerved. They tried to avoid looking at one another. Staring intently at the floor, as if searching for something, some passengers tried to act normal, hoping for the flight to take off soon. Finally, there sounded the announcement for the take-off. A well-dressed Sinhala woman stood at the entrance, welcoming each traveller and permitting them to pass through. A fringe of hair fell over her forehead, hiding her eyes. Comparing the photograph in every passport against the face of its respective passenger, she handed over all the documents before sending them off. When my turn came, she checked my papers and wished me a pleasant journey. Keep your country to yourself, I have got a new one, I thought, and smiled.

I was surprised that Musa, who usually licked me, had bitten me on that day. The overcoat had transformed me. It could be a bad omen, as my mother had feared. The charismatic man whom I had guessed was a teacher sat at a distance, reading a newspaper. I was anxious but didn't know why. I remembered the jeans-clad girl and the officials dragging her away, even as she cried that it wasn't her. It was distressing to see her begging like an illiterate village woman. She had appeared so civil and educated. What error could she have made? Could it have been a fake passport? Or was she a freedom fighter? The hope in her eyes! I remembered her confident walk, with the bag slung on her shoulders. I had two glasses of wine after the flight took off from Karachi, and forgot about the incident. I fell asleep, and when I woke up, we had arrived in Moscow.

TWO

New Agent

A frail-looking person met us at the Sheremetyevo airport in Moscow. His was the first Russian name I encountered. It was quite a mouthful, I thought, and said it to myself three times to get the pronunciation right. The organiser identified all eight people and gathered them. I had already guessed who some of them were. The charismatic person was indeed a teacher. But when he introduced himself as Ambikapathi, I thought—what kind of name is this, this name doesn't suit his persona.

I said, 'I am Nishant.'

The one I couldn't hazard a guess about was a middle-aged woman. The others called her Chandra mami, meaning aunty. The rest were all young. Rohan—a Sinhalese youth—was a surprise element. The agent packed us all into a vehicle and checked us into a low-budget hotel.

Over the next few days, we were to travel to Ukraine by train. I wanted to see Moscow a little bit, but that was not to be. What I saw of Russia was only through the windows of the hotel. Even now, Russia, to me, means that first sight I witnessed in Moscow from the hotel window. I never forgot it.

It must have been about eight in the evening. I stood watching from my window. Every scene seemed novel. The vehicles plying on the roads, the trees on the sidewalk—they were all exotic and strange. Even the birds there were ones I had never seen before. The men and women walked briskly, as if chasing after something. It was bitterly cold and everyone was in overcoats. The images of people were sharp and distinct when they passed by streetlights, and then changed into silhouettes as they moved further away.

I saw a woman of about fifty on the street, in a black overcoat, black hat and black gloves. Suddenly, a car hit her, throwing her upwards, where she hung suspended in the air for a few seconds, before landing on the road with a thud. Chandra mami, standing next to me, cried aloud. It was like watching a giant bird flapping its wings and flying across. For a few moments, I was too shocked to respond. My brain turned numb. I couldn't see any more after that as a crowd had gathered around the victim. What happened next was even more astounding. In barely two minutes, an ambulance arrived, alarms blaring, and took the woman away. The street returned to normalcy. The people who had crowded around walked away. All traces of the accident vanished. For several years after that, I was reminded of this scene whenever I thought of Moscow.

When everything settled down, Ambikapathi master said, 'You don't have to read the newspapers to know how a government functions. Even more unnecessary is to listen to a radio or watch the television. A scene like this is enough.'

For six days, we remained confined to the hotel—as if in a prison. On the seventh day, four people—Ambikapathi master, Chandra mami, Rohan and I—were to board a train to Ukraine, where another agent, who spoke Russian, would take charge of us.

Ambikapathi master, who was headed to France, while everyone else had chosen Canada, took a look at the dog bite when I was applying medicine on my calf. 'It is a domesticated dog, nothing to worry about. It will heal before we reach Ukraine,' he said. Just as he had said, by the time we left for Ukraine, the wound had healed.

'Master, how do you stay so calm?'

'I learnt from my students, Nishant. Two of them are in Paris, and I'm going to see them. Six students joined the liberation movement one after another. Holding me responsible, the Sinhala army came looking for me. I was forced to leave the country. A student called Bageerathan often said that he did not fear death. If that was true, I told him, the theory of evolution was false. Every living being has three primal emotions: hunger, fear and lust. Bageerathan would say, death is like crossing a threshold. There are many who thought the same way. On the day of his hanging, Bhagat Singh was racing through a book on Lenin. He was hanged before he could finish the first chapter. Bhagat Singh was more worried about finishing the book than death.

'Bageerathan's friend was hit by a bomb during the war, which fell into the enemy's military zone. Bageerathan crawled into the enemy territory and drew his friend's body outside even as bullets were flying in all directions. He did not fear for his life. It was his belief that when doing what you think is right, you won't be afraid of death. He performed his friend's funeral.

'There was great truth in his statement. There was a similar scene in Sophocles' play *Antigone*. Antigone's brother had died in a war and, according to the king's order, the body was not to be buried and sanctified with sacred funeral rites.

While burying Polyneices in secret, Antigone was caught and produced before the king. Antigone argued that the law of God was more powerful than that of the king's. When the king punished her, she was unafraid of death. She showed no fear of death while standing by truth.

'We don't travel to the world of the dead. We travel from one country to another. That's it. We achieve nothing by being tense. Buddha attained enlightenment only when he was at peace. There's no use getting worked up. We should train ourselves to be calm,' Ambikapathi master said.

The Ukraine agent Vijayanayagam wasn't someone who inspired hope, but they said he was knowledgeable. The apartment he got us there was on the eighth floor of a tall building. Four people were already living in it. It had a bathroom, a bedroom and a kitchen. So, once again, there was eight of us. One of the four living there from before we arrived was called Padmarasan. His was a name that everyone in Jaffna knew. There was talk—which he did not refute—that he had been involved in a bank robbery. He had escaped and landed here. Upon inquiry, the name of the Sinhalese boy Rohan turned out to be even more well known in Colombo. He had been caught raping a student from Vishaka School and had somehow managed to escape. Back in Colombo, the police were still looking for him.

For six days in Moscow, we hadn't had a decent meal. Vijayanayagam, probably moved by our pitiful sight, bought us four pounds of bread, two dozen eggs and some milk. In Russian, bread is called khleb. It's the second Russian word I learnt. The third word was moloko, meaning milk. The eggs bought by the agent were twice as big as the ones found in

Colombo. The bread loaf came whole, unsliced. Somehow, we managed to tear it up and share it.

There was a gas stove and a frying pan in the kitchen. And a woman who knew how to cook: Chandra mami. She fried two eggs for each person. We lined up to get our share of fried eggs and bread, which we ate while standing. Only starving animals can eat so fast. Not one person left anything uneaten on their plate. Then we drank Ukrainian water and said it was the most wonderful meal we had ever had.

The apartment had a telephone, which hung in the bathroom—a common area. Relatives and friends of agents from various countries used to call on this number. Most of the calls were complaints. Sometimes, they carried messages of hope. If a Russian caller came on the line, the agent would speak to them in Russian. Sometimes, during the conversation, he would laugh like a Russian too. We heard that this agent was able to send off his clients faster because he knew Russian. He would come once in the morning and once in the evening. He never answered questions but had plenty of questions to ask us.

Sammandhan, who had been here for three months now, apprised me of what had happened before his group came to Ukraine. His path hadn't yet opened. One morning, the agent had taken away two young men staying with him. They must have been from the liberation movement. Hardly seventeen or eighteen, they were muscular and spoke not a word of English. They always stuck together, and it was mentioned in hushed tones that both had had a role in the assassination of the Sri Lankan defence minister, Ranjan Wijeratne. For two years, they had lived with cyanide capsules hanging round their necks. 'If someone had so many ways to die, how many ways could there be to live?' they would often ask. Two days later, the telephone in the bathroom rang and those two youths spoke from Canada. Everyone began to believe that the agent had magical powers; he would redeem us all.

That night, we slept on the plastic mats on which over a hundred people had surely slept before. I slept between the bank robber, who covered himself with a long cloth, and Rohan, the Sinhalese youth who had raped a thirteen-year-old school girl. I could hear their breathing. They were both drooling. The sounds outside were different. The nightbirds sounded like they were in distress. I remembered Chandra mami mentioning the name of the bird. The air carried a different scent. Sometime in the future, I would be holding in my hand a new, dark blue passport as a permanent citizen of either the UK, Germany or Canada. But tonight, I was breathing the same air that had earlier been inhaled by Tolstoy, Chekhov, Turgenev, Lenin, Stalin and Gorbachev. I did not know what the future held. I had been born in Kuppilan in Sri Lanka, but my death was bound to happen in a different country. Born on 16 December under the star Rohini, I had weighed six pounds at birth. Nobody could alter these facts. Not even the mighty Sri Lankan army.

Before falling asleep, my last memory was of my girlfriend, Divya. We had been in love for two years, and she was very fond of being constantly 'rescued' by me. She had left me for a boy from the movement, Suresh. Did he make a good lover just because he wore a military uniform and carried a K-56 rifle made in China?

The next morning, I woke three hours after sunrise. Neither the bank robber nor the child rapist was going to wake me up. Amma wouldn't stand in front of me, holding a cup of coffee. My sister wasn't going to kick me playfully while passing by. I had pinned all my hopes on the agent who spoke Russian. But I was unaware that he would soon sell me off.

THREE

Fire Service

I did not see the sunrise in Ukraine on my first day and woke up only after the sun had captured the sky. The very sound and smell of the air was different—I could tell even with my eyes closed. By the time I awoke, the rest had washed up by turns and were waiting. I could see that everyone had something to worry about. Master was reading something and Mami was uttering a prayer. I remembered how agent Vijayanayagam had once remarked that being a refugee meant 'waiting'. We were waiting as if something important was bound to happen that day. We didn't know that for a whole month nothing would happen, that soon we would start thinking that jail might have been better than this uncertain waiting.

On a night when six of us were in the apartment, the Russian-speaking agent called and asked us to sit down on the floor. He said that Chandra mami, Master and I were to stay back and be taken care of by another agent. The rest had to prepare to leave the next morning. I was shocked. I looked at Chandra mami. She was looking away, through the window, at birds on a tree, as though completely disconnected from current events. Master was not so shocked.

'Master, this is not fair. We paid the same amount of money. Amma raised it by selling our land. We cannot be treated like this ... Is there nobody who can protest against this injustice?' I ranted.

That night, Master comforted me.

'We have no clue how they operate. But they will certainly take us to a new country somehow. Don't worry.'

'No, Master, they are selling us off like they would damaged goods. If a new agent doesn't show tomorrow, we will end up begging on the streets.'

'That won't happen to you. Those who are leaving aren't going to achieve anything by going a day earlier. Everything happens according to some pre-written destiny. You won't understand it today, but maybe someday you will.'

The next day, three people left with the agent. 'A new agent will reach here this evening. He is more experienced than I am. Not to worry,' said the agent as he left. I was furious that we were being abandoned in an unfamiliar country, in a language environment that we did not understand. But I drew comfort from Master's words.

When the doorbell rang at night, my heart leapt in excitement. I hadn't the slightest idea about the shock that was waiting on the other side of the door. The new agent had brought five more people. It was difficult to identify him in an overcoat and hat, which he removed when he stepped inside. The shock I got on recognising him was indescribable. I remembered my mother's cries pleading for me to not go after the dog-bite, which she had seen as a bad omen. My head spun, thinking in how many more ways God would test me again and again.

Because the agent who arrived was none other than Jumper! The man who had told me in the restaurant back in Colombo that he had had no time on that day to kill me. How he had turned into an agent was a mystery. Seeing him, I thought my life was over. But Jumper looked like he had forgotten everything. He issued orders to those who had accompanied him. His appearance and manner inspired some hope.

The five people he had brought were somewhat unique. There was a powerfully built man who could be around forty. They said he was a dentist. The others included a young Sinhalese called Kaluwella, a sixty-year-old man named Mohan, a teenager, and a young woman who lit up the room. The agent addressed her as Lavanya. She was the first to smile at me. Unaware of the cold climate in Ukraine until then, she wore a sleeveless dress. In no time, she began to shiver and covered her shoulders with her hands. Her eyes were shaded by locks of hair, which she was constantly pushing aside. Educated at Vembadi school, she was now preparing to go to Paris.

One day I asked her what she intended to do in Paris. When she said 'fashion design', I wondered if there were educational courses for such things.

Later that day, when Jumper rushed in, she murmured that trouble was coming. But he had brought good news. He had found a way out for Master. They wouldn't let refugees live together for long, fearing that they would bond and hesitate to leave each other. For me, it was devastating news, yet I was happy for Master.

'How will I survive without you?' I asked Master.

'Have you grown dependant on me? This friendship is temporary. You need to trust yourself.'

It had been a month since we had arrived in Ukraine. We had to plan every exit. Patience was the most important trait a refugee had to cultivate. Boiling water would eventually cool down. However high it flew, a bird had to make a landing. It was important to practise patience.

'I didn't mean that. Just as *Virakesari* newspaper asks the readers to jump to page number 5, then to 8 and then to 11, they toss us around to different agents. You will reach early. What about us? When do we start? When will we reach?'

'Brother, we shouldn't be thinking of who will reach earlier or later. Once there was a strong, four-winged bird. This is not a story, it's a scientific truth. The birds that lived 130 million years ago were called microraptors. Two-winged birds were their meal! They hunted down two-winged birds. To survive, the two-winged birds had to fly harder. The four-winged birds couldn't catch them. They starved and eventually died. It is not about earlier or later. What matters is talent and presence of mind. One should be able to constantly adapt to changing circumstances. Darwin called it survival of the fittest. A refugee in search of a new country should have this basic understanding.'

Compared to Chandra mami, Mohan was carefree. He looked gullible too. He had three-tier teeth. Without any hesitation, he addressed Lavanya as 'akka', elder sister. She was talkative. When talking to me one day, she said that she liked my face, I couldn't understand what she meant. I thought about it the whole night. A woman who planned to study fashion design in Paris liked my face. Could she also like my elbows? What about my feet? Would she like every part of me?

Jumper, our new agent, was someone who made impulsive decisions. By watching whom he talked to, no one could tell how he arrived at the decisions. Early one morning, he asked Master to get ready to leave.

'Right away?'

'Are you here as a tourist? A refugee's time is in his agent's hands. He decides on a time that will suit a particular exit and work best for you. Don't question me.'

Master dumped all his essentials in a shoulder bag and left. The others felt cheated. They rejoiced for him but were otherwise sad. Besides, it was a mystery why Lavanya, Mohan or I weren't chosen. Even though the agent had already answered the question. He knew which path would suit which refugee. Could he do this job without that kind of knowledge?

Master bade everyone farewell. 'I'm not sure where I am headed. Do we have any choice but to dance to their tunes? Even if they push me into the sea, nobody can question them. If I do reach a country, I will write to you. The letter could also arrive from the prison of a strange country. But it will arrive! Do not go to another country before it does,' he told me, hugged and left hastily.

There was no word from him for the next week. No one spoke about it but spent all their time glancing at the telephone. When it rang, everybody ran towards it. But it was finally the agent who attended the call and smiled as he announced, 'Master has reached Canada.' But hadn't he wanted to go to Paris? Though difficult to believe, the truth was that from the start, Master had wanted to go to Paris but had ended up in Canada.

After a month passed, a letter arrived for me with a stamp carrying the image of a big-horned moose from the province of Alberta in Canada. Master had written about his journey to Canada. I passed it around for the others to read.

'Don't underestimate the agent. If someone asked you about the meeting point of two ships operating at different speeds and sailing in different directions at sea, you might use your mathematical reasoning and find the answer. If someone asked me what Jack London's first story was, I would answer them without any hesitation. I could even narrate the story. But that brand of intellect is useless to the agent. His brains are filled with wisdom on survival, which is needed in this world. I will tell you the story of how I reached Canada. You might not believe it.

'The agent sent me to a country I couldn't have imagined visiting in all my life. Cuba. I touched Turkey, then flew to Brazil, and from there reached Cuba. But why Cuba? Because you don't need a visa to go there. I stayed at a cheap lodge. Ernest Hemmingway had once lived in this country. A writer who met with many accidents. When his plane caught fire, he ended up reading the news about his death. He wrote The Old Man and the Sea *in Cuba and won the Nobel Prize. The house where he lived and wrote from was nearby. But I had been ordered not to step out, so I couldn't see the house he had lived in. I got a ticket for Guatemala. A representative of the agent called to instruct me about the time and place for the flight. Guatemala doesn't need visas either, I had no idea. So, I handed over my ticket, went to the airport lounge, and waited for the flight, boarding pass in hand.*

'A miracle happened next. A seventeen- or eighteen-year-old Tamil youth came up to me and said, "Brother, no questions. Hand me your boarding pass to Guatemala. Take my boarding pass to Canada and board the flight. Once you land there, you can seek refugee status and they will accept you." I asked him how he would manage. "I hold a Canadian passport; I will go to Guatemala and fly to Canada from there," he said and walked towards the flight bound for Guatemala.

I reached Canada without any problem. The Canadian official at Immigration gave me a warm welcome.

'So, you can blindly trust the agent. He will somehow get you into a country.'

Lavanya always looked cheerful. She'd smile after speaking or talk after smiling. One day, she was seated on the floor, with her head resting on her knees and chin on her chest. Her hands were on her head. It was evident that she was distressed. All other residents had gone out, and she alone was left behind with me.

'What are you thinking about?'

'Master's story is terrifying. Had he been caught at some airport, Master would have written his letter from some jail. The agent never said any of this when I set out. I thought he would take us in a group. But he's sending everyone separately. How will I manage? Can't he send us together? If I travel with you, I won't worry.'

'It would be good if we travelled together. Even otherwise, we'll stay in touch. If you leave early, you can write to me. If I leave before you, I'll write to you,' I responded.

She was silent.

'You'll write, won't you?' I asked her.

'Of course,' she promised. 'Who else will I write to?'

Jumper, who always sulked, came sporting a rare smile that day. Rice was barely ever cooked in our kitchen. Normally, we cooked wheat puttu. Mami had cooked rice along with chicken curry that day. Jumper ate with us.

I thought this was a good time to ask. 'It's kind of intimidating when you send people individually. Can't you send us as a team? We could help each other on the way, feel safer.'

Jumper turned pensive. His face was like a sharpened pencil. His eyes closed. He pointed to the clothes that had been hung to dry from a line tied to a window grille at one end and a pillar at the other. On that clothesline were Mami's sari and blouse, Mohan's T-shirt and jeans, Lavanya's skirt and my pants and shirt. 'All the clothes washed together are being dried here. But they don't dry out the same way. Jeans take up to two days to dry. A T-shirt will take only four hours. A sari takes about eight hours. There is a reason why things take time. A travel plan designed for you will not suit Mami. I take everything into consideration while chalking out your routes and times of departure. You should trust me without question.'

'But not knowing what to expect is making us anxious,' I said.

'You all are like fire-service men. You should always be on red alert. Haven't you spent money to find asylum in another country? Is finding a safe country child's play? You must always stay prepared, like a doctor working in a war camp.'

Even when Lavanya's mouth was closed, a tiny attractive gap showed between her lips. She wore anklets that made noise round the clock. They gave away her location like a GPS system.

'What is fashion designing?' I asked her one day.

'Do any of us wear what the primitive men wore? Isn't there progress in mankind's dressing? Fashion design is a course about that.'

She probably thought this explanation would suffice for me. She was happy that I had asked. Her eyes danced like two hanging lamps. After some hesitation, I told her, 'I like your lips.' She opened the lips and smiled. The same smile she had offered to Mohan. The same smile she had offered to Mami and to Jumper.

I wondered how her parents could have trusted her with someone like Jumper. Among us all, Mohan was the youngest. His face looked as if someone had wiped all intelligence off it with a cloth. He trusted everyone. On entering the apartment, Jumper would hand him a chicken and tell him to leave it in the kitchen sink. Mohan would play with the chicken by throwing it up and catching it until he reached the kitchen. His elder brother lived in Germany. He said his brother was very rich.

'What does he do?' I had asked him one day.

'He owns nineteen ATM machines. You can withdraw any amount of money any time.'

Lavanya hid her laughter with her hand and looked at me. I looked at Mami. Then Lavanya and I laughed uncontrollably. Mohan joined us and laughed out loud. Mami laughed as well. Everyone laughed, but for different reasons. Lavanya laughing uncontrollably holding her stomach was a sight to relish.

It was the last time we all laughed together.

FOUR

The Luxury of a Mat

I remembered my mother's wish that I visit Red Square in Moscow. She had also mentioned the remains of Vladimir Lenin, which had been preserved in a museum. Her list also had the Victory Circle constructed in memory of Russia's triumph over Napoleon. But I could see none of these places. The agent locked us into a cheap hotel room. I knew that red flags with a hammer on the left and a sickle on the right flew atop buildings in Moscow. But my wish to see them did not come to pass, either; the flag changed after the collapse of the Soviet Union.

It was hard to suppress the disappointment at my inability to see anything of the famous city of Moscow though I had stayed there for six days.

'Are you tourists?' Jumper would ask angrily whenever I expressed a desire to go see the sights in Ukraine. He looked as if some evil thought was threading through his mind.

What could we refugees do? Had we elected him? In fact, *he* had chosen us. In the last six months, I had tried to cross the border into Poland twice and, on both occasions, been caught and sent back. When sixteen-year-old Mohan was caught, they caned him till his back bled.

The owner of the apartment—a woman—lived on the ninth floor. The rent Jumper gave her was her only source of income. She was utterly unaware of what was happening around her. She would probably believe it if someone told her that the Second World War was still on. She distilled a type of vodka called Samogon at home. You will know the strength and taste of it only if you drink it, Jumper would say.

I would often go to the owner's house to learn Russian. Her late husband had worked as a dentist during the Soviet Union era. In broken English, she would speak about the teeth her husband had extracted and even showed me some that were preserved in a glass box, as mementoes. Sometimes, she would offer a glass of Samogon. Then, like the warriors of the past, she would pour a drop of her home-distilled liquor into my glass and then we would drink together. If she was happy, she would raise the back of her skirt with both hands and do a troika, a dance that imitates the prancing of a horse pulling a carriage.

Chandra mami was an avid reader. She spent most of her time with books. She was also a keen observer of nature. Her late husband had been a professor in Colombo, and she was on her way to her daughter in France. Her husband had often told her, 'Read the Bible or Shakespeare; if you can't read either, read *Animal Farm*.' After her husband's death, she started reading that book on a sleepless night and finished it before dawn. She realised that this wasn't the type of book to read when trying to fall asleep.

'What's it about?' I asked.

'It's just a hundred pages, but it speaks about all of human life. The animals once voted on whether rats were good or bad. The dogs and cats couldn't decide, and said they were good and bad at the same time. This is the human game, thambi,' she said. I'm not sure I understood that. I nodded both ways.

Chandra mami used to wake up very early. Sometimes, I too would be early to rise. The room would be filled with the odour of feet. I would drink the tea she prepared. Chandra mami would often walk around the building. Sometimes, I joined her. She would keenly observe the trees and identify them by name—oak, elm, ash. She once told me that there were five hundred types of butterflies in the neighbourhood. She'd get excited as a child, watching them. The sight of birds made her delirious. Once, when I said that a sparrow was squeaking in distress, I saw Chandra mami's annoyance for the first time. 'That's not it at all,' she said and added, 'it's singing.' She showed me the black-headed, white-breasted sparrow with grey wings hiding in the trees. 'However cold it gets, this bird doesn't migrate. In winters, it reduces its own body heat.'

One day, when the agent said we could leave, I inquired about the route. But my question fell on deaf ears. Instead, Jumper urged us to get ready.

Thiyagarajan had already warned me not to leave without inquiring about the route. He had failed several times to cross the border by trusting the agent. Our six-member group was handed over to two Pakistanis. There were a total of eight people travelling. I decided to go only because the group also included Chandra mami. But I resolved to turn back halfway if the path turned out to be fraught with danger.

The journey began in two Lada Zhiguli cars, elongated in the front and at the back. I tried talking to the Pakistanis, but they responded only in monosyllables. After four hours of travel, I was able to ascertain where the cars were headed. The plan was to travel to Belarus, and from there, across the border of Lithuania to Poland and then on to Germany. It was a dangerous route. I had heard that if caught, the police at the borders would not hesitate to smash our heads in. We were dropped near a woods and handed a pencil-sized torch each. We had to travel through the dark, holding each other's hands. Mohan held my jacket and Chandra mami, the last person in the group, gripped Mohan's hands. I decided not to hold hands and to turn back before reaching the light from the camp at the border.

When a big tree blocked our path, I hid behind it. Mohan and Chandra mami were not aware of anything. Unfamiliar with directions, we stepped into a marshland in the dark. A fine light emanated from the pencil torch. As we kept walking, the water rose to our knees. There were trees all around. We suddenly crashed against a fallen tree in the dark. But then we got past it and kept staggering forward. Yet we couldn't find which side land was on. Suddenly Chandra mami said, 'These are tropical trees. I can hear the sound of water birds. The land should be in the opposite direction.' She was right. When we walked in the opposite direction, we found land. But a huge branch of the fallen tree that we had crashed into had pierced Chandra mami's thigh, and she dropped to the ground, crying. As blood oozed from her injury, daylight broke.

We were soaking wet. Walking even a step forward became an ordeal. Mami was writhing in pain. I thought a piece of the branch had broken inside her thigh. We wrapped her in a blanket pulled out of my backpack and carried her, often breaking for a rest. The morning rushed towards noon. Mami was sometimes awake, sometimes dizzy. And at one point, she said, 'Brothers, leave me here. It is useless for me to escape! Is the mayor of Kiev going to give the city's key to me?'

'We struggled so hard to carry you up till here, just to abandon you?' I firmly refused.

When a bird flew very close over my head, I knew that we had reached the main road. Stopping a random car, I said in broken Russian that we needed to go to Kiev. For a fee of $100, the driver agreed. All along the journey, Chandra mami continued to moan in pain. Upon returning to the apartment in Kiev, the agent paid the driver without asking any questions and sent him back. When I told him that we were lost in the woods and that the others had crossed the border, the agent cursed the Pakistanis for an entire day for abandoning us.

On the fifth day after our return, there was a knock on the door at dinner time. We looked through the keyhole, worried that it could be the police. But to our amazement, it was those five people who we thought had crossed the border successfully. The two Pakistanis did not raise their heads. Their faces were dark, worn out, and bore marks of dried blood; their shirts were torn. They hadn't just been beaten at the border but had also lost their money and been treated like labourers—forced to carry bricks. Hearing of their ordeal, I felt a spurt of satisfaction deep down.

Chandra mami's health continued to deteriorate, and so, she had to be admitted to a hospital. A big chunk of the broken branch was surgically removed from her thigh, and in a few days, she was sent home. Blood oozed into a small plastic container hanging from the tube the doctors had inserted into the wound. It was mandatory to note in a book the quantity of blood collected in the container when dressing the wound every day: 18 ml on Monday, 24 ml on Tuesday, 19 ml on Wednesday, etc., and the notes had to be handed over to the doctor on the weekends. Only then would he prescribe the medicines for the following week. I did the job with utmost commitment.

One day, when I was measuring the blood, Chandra mami started to weep uncontrollably.

'I don't know who your parents are. You struggle so much for me. Leave me, thambi. I will die here.'

'Why are you talking like this, mami—we couldn't abandon you.'

'There's an old poem, brother. It starts like this: *Who is your mother? Who is your father? What is between us?* You were born somewhere and I, somewhere else. How did we meet here in Ukraine, in this small city of Kiev? Why should you serve me like this? How will I ever repay you?' She broke down again.

'What is this, mami? You are such a courageous woman. Don't you often say that we should live each day like it's our last?' I said.

'It will soon be true,' she murmured.

The thigh had turned septic, so the doctors had to cut off the remaining gangrened flesh. Still, mami would make tea every morning, limping. One day she did not get up. When asked why, she said, 'The plastic mat won the day.' Her situation worsened. The doctors couldn't diagnose what was wrong with her.

Christmas was celebrated on 7 January in Ukraine. The owner of the flat sent us the traditionally prepared twelve-course meal. According to the belief there, the twelve types of food were for the twelve apostles of Jesus. Mami enjoyed the special meal and was particularly happy on that day.

But nobody foresaw what happened next. The agent couldn't bear mami's crying in pain in the middle of the night.

'Jesus died hanging on the Cross. Don't you have the luxury of a mat? What is your problem? Why do you wail and spoil our sleep?'

How could such cruel words escape the agent's lips? Tears streamed down mami's cheeks. From that day on, she barely drank any water, let alone eat anything. She lay like a discarded log of wood. Having lost weight, bones protruded from unexpected places in her body. While she kept repeating her daughter's name, her memory grew feeble.

Everybody took turns to be by mami's side. Her world had shrunk, and the only sound we heard from her was her breathing. I would often call out—'mami … mami …', but her eyes remained closed. One morning, the sun's rays crept into the house, forming a fine line. The trees came to life and some sparrows sang.

'Mami, can you hear the sparrow?'

'It's not a sparrow. It's a loon, a water bird. It has returned from migration. Today is the day,' she said, enunciating every word clearly. Her eyes were not open though, and in a few moments, she was dead.

I had no idea what her last words—today is the day—meant.

FIVE

Give Me Your Heart

It was no use ringing the bell. I banged on the door with my hands and then kicked it. Silence. The new agent refused to open the door.

Then, a minute after the door opened, Ravi's face popped out. Then the face disappeared when I started speaking, and the closed door stared at me. I banged on the door again, but it remained shut.

'Return my money, or send me back home,' I yelled.

The words spoken in Tamil disappeared one by one into thin air. There was no one in the vicinity in Ukraine who understood my words.

This was a day to remember my mother. Two years had passed since I left home and I was still in Ukraine. My sister who set off after me had already reached Canada. I never read more than two lines when Amma's letters arrived. I would read the next two lines later.

'I taught my class about Russia yesterday. I was thinking of you. The students don't know that you are still there. I remember how we shared the same body for nine months. It is a comforting thought. I

made your favourite nethili fish curry yesterday. But I couldn't eat a morsel.'

I tried to remember Amma's face. The image of Amma sitting in a corner under a light and knitting a blanket shone in my memory. She would count the stitches and undo everything if she missed a single one. That image—of her sitting alone, counting and knitting again—would leave me unsettled. Amma hadn't thought twice about selling her land to pay the agent. How easy the agent had made it all sound! 'Oh, no problem in reaching Ukraine!'

Poland was another border away from Ukraine. Germany was one more border away from Poland. Relatives in Germany had promised Amma to take care of me when I reached there.

Jumper had sold us off to Ravi, the new agent. Sent off by Ravi, I was caught for a third time at the Polish border. My hair was frozen, making rustling sounds when I combed it. I had stuffed newspapers between my chest and the first layer of clothing, to keep the cold out. The officials chased me off—*Thavaai, Thavaai*. They laughed at my protective cover of newspapers when searching me. I was beaten till the skin on my back came off in strips. As they tossed me around, I realised that I was only an object of fun. The very thought of that pain sends shivers down my spine even now.

Two people could be created by melting Ravi who was tall and thickset. He had a scar on his neck and a mole on his cheek, like villains in Tamil movies. He always carried a travel bag, but no one had seen him open it. He claimed to have sent two hundred people to different destinations. He often boasted: 'Like the rear-view mirror of a car, I can see what's coming behind me. That's why I'm successful!'

One day, Ravi brought four new people: Eswari, her child Laila, Chellathambi and Alex. After their arrival, the average IQ of those in apartment number 808 was reduced by half. It was easy to guess that Chellathambi had been dropped from the movement. He walked holding himself at an angle, shoulders quivering. He would open his mouth wide and yell as if he was talking to someone in the next village. At first glance, he appeared dull, but his brain worked systematically. An official had asked him for his age as soon as he landed in Ukraine.

'Should I answer today?' he asked.

His story spread fast among the refugees in Ukraine. On the second day of his arrival, though he did not know a word of Russian, he cut a hundred metres of telephone wire and sold it off. It was a continuing mystery as to how he managed to sell pretty much anything in a country totally foreign to him. Once, he stole an old woman's hearing aid and even asked for advice on whom he should sell it to. Another time, he managed to catch a rabbit and make a curry out of it. In Ukraine, rabbits are white in winter and turn brown in summer. This one was white.

'You cannot catch a rabbit by chasing it. To catch a rabbit, you have to think like it. You will have to guess where it will head to and wait there,' he said, when people enquired about his feat.

Meanwhile, Ravi refused to indulge me. He kept asking for more money. I had to borrow money from my sister who had reached Canada. What a disgrace! She sent 1400 dollars to Ravi. It was after this that the 'Ramesh' incident occurred. At one point in time, every Tamil refugee in Ukraine knew of the incident. Ravi handed me a brand new passport. It wasn't a fake but an original Sri Lankan passport. It had many visa stamps on it. Ravi's people had replaced the photograph on the passport with mine. Now my name was Ramesh Sivaprakasam, and I was nineteen years old. I memorised everything in the passport as I would travel on it. Four Russians had agreed to take me to Poland.

'They will be here by 11 a.m. Be ready,' Ravi had said and left.

I woke up the next morning, took a bath and got dressed. I could carry a small shoulder bag. The Russians rushed in at ten. They were early by an hour. I was still in the bathroom. There was another Ramesh in the apartment, also a refugee. His full name was Ramesh Karunakaran. When the Russians called out, 'Ramesh!', he picked up his bag and left with them. When I emerged from the bathroom, the others laughed at me. I couldn't believe it. Was it possible for a refugee to deceive another refugee? Ravi had no idea what had happened. Neither did the Russians. When they came and asked for 'Ramesh', the other Ramesh had left with them.

Shamed, humiliated and disappointed, I did not step out of the house, or even get off the mat once I lay down on it. When Ravi realised what had happened, he scolded me. But two days later, when they heard the news, Ravi was the first to be shocked. The Russians were part of a drug mafia. They would hurl drug packets across the border, and the gang members on the other side, in Poland, would pick them up. But in the process, they had lost some packets. So, they needed a mule to get the drugs across. When they were caught, they made a scapegoat of Ramesh Karunakaran who could do nothing to save himself. He didn't know the language either, to be able to say anything in his own defence. He was sentenced to six years' rigorous imprisonment. In

Poland, rigorous imprisonment meant sheer torture. The prisoner was kept in a dark cell. But when counting the years of the sentence, the prisons there would count the day as one day and night as another. This way, Ramesh Karunakaran's punishment would end in three years instead of six.

'Did he not cheat you? Let him suffer,' Ravi had said.

After three months, I received a letter from Ramesh from a Polish jail. The letter had only four lines. Since he had written in the dark, the lines were uneven. *'Forgive me. I am suffering for my dishonesty. You are a good person. I am, in fact, happy that I've been sentenced to this punishment in your place.'* The letter upset me. Someone else was suffering what I might have. But there were other worries that made me forget this.

Poove Poochoodavaa was the first Tamil film that I watched in a Ukrainian theatre. It was funny to watch Padmini and Nadhiya speak Russian on the big screen. The reception it got in Russia was unimaginable. Russian women were weeping as they watched.

Some new refugees would sometimes bring movie videos with them. *Ullathai Alli Thaa* (Give Me Your Heart) was one of them. Famous stars like Karthik and Rambha acted in the movie. The refugees played the video cassette every evening after dinner. The high point of the movie was the song *'Azhagiya Laila'*, a raging hit at the time. In the song, Rambha danced in a short skirt, with a fan blowing her skirt up and baring her thighs.

Eswari was a slim, attractive woman. She and her daughter were waiting to join her husband in France. But in the few months that she had already spent in Ukraine, she had become less interested in going to France. She would wash her hair in the morning and strut around like a princess in a flowing gown, with her hair cascading on either side as she dried it. Alex, who had travelled with them from Colombo, hardly looked like a refugee. He had long hair, which he used to fasten with a rubber band. He didn't smoke Maltovo like the others; his choice were the luxurious Marlboro cigarettes. He and Eswari conversed with each other in whispers, making sure no one heard them. She would bend her head towards him, as he listened keenly, and laugh aloud at all his jokes. If someone intruded, she would draw back, as if she'd been pushed away. Eswari was teaching her four-year-old daughter Laila to dance to *Azhagiya Laila*. The child danced well, just like Rambha, swirling her waist, moving her eyes around and kicking her legs. In fact, Rambha could probably learn a step or two from Laila!

One evening, Alex dusted the sofa for Eswari to sit on, and though there was enough space, Alex sat very close to her. Laila stood wearing a short skirt, just like Rambha, ready to dance. Exactly at that moment, the telephone rang. Four people ran towards it. It was an ill-timed call from Eswari's husband in France. Extending the wire from the bathroom, I handed over the receiver to Eswari, but she signalled to me to not give her the phone. Instead of talking to her husband, Eswari played the tape recorder and the child began to dance. Alex was lying on the floor with a fan by his side, and he operated it in such a way as to blow the child's skirt upwards. The skirt kept flying up, and everyone applauded. Eswari's eyes glowed with pride. For a moment, Eswari and Alex exchanged furtive glances.

'Aren't you ashamed? Your husband is waiting to talk to you and you are making your child perform a disgraceful dance?' I asked.

'Who are you to say so?' asked Alex, standing up.

I lashed out and landed a blow. As Alex fell to the floor, he struck his cheek on the corner of a table and lay bleeding. Even as everyone else stared, Chellathambi rushed Alex to the hospital. Those who saw him running said he was as swift as a white rabbit. Alex got four sutures on his cheek.

Probably this was the reason why Ravi wasn't opening the door. He disapproved of my hitting Alex. I wandered aimlessly on the road. I came upon a railway crossing. After which came the chestnut trees that stood in a row, their tops covered in pink flowers. The park was serene when I entered it. I wondered why I shouldn't kill myself there. This way, I wouldn't have to beg Ravi for a way out every morning. How wonderful—to be born in a small village like Kuppilan and die in Ukraine!

There was a time when the name Laura filled me with hope and happiness. She would visit the flat owner on the ninth floor. I met her often. Everything about me surprised her. I told her I was a 'refugee', but she did not understand what it meant. As if solving a very hard mathematical problem, she kept asking me for an explanation. Finally, she saw the meaning in an English-Russian dictionary and laughed, and then kept laughing. I was incensed that she was laughing at my plight.

'A person without parents is an orphan. A person without a country is a refugee. Can't you get even this?' I asked her.

'Forgive me,' she said and kissed me. That was her first kiss.

She was very playful and impatient. Our love blossomed in a very short time and died for a very trivial reason. The plan was that I would go to Germany and then invite her there. But Ramesh Karunakaran spoiled the plan. She was angry. 'You aren't in love with me. You are just preparing me to be your wife,' she told me and broke up. It was rumoured that she was back with her old boyfriend now.

My sister would have toiled hard to send 1400 dollars for me to pay Ravi, but he was so heartless. He said I could no longer live in flat number 808.

Three trains passed through the railway crossing every day. I was waiting for the noon train. It was the beginning of April. The morning calls of birds filled the skies. The sun hid between clouds, granting only a little light to the earth. It would take another three hours for it to reach its zenith. I calculated the time in my village at that moment. Amma would have finished her first class after lunch. When teaching about Europe, she would talk about the Central Uplands. She would teach about coniferous and deciduous forests, which I could not picture in my mind back then when I was in school. I thought of Amma now when I came across coniferous forests in Ukraine. I thought I would be dead by the time Amma finished her classes. Who would break the news to her? Would they bury me without informing her of my death? Would my sister travel from Canada to see my body? How much would she need for a flight ticket? Would she have to wash 20,000 plates and cups to raise that kind of money?

I happened to notice an old man sitting on the track, a little distance away. I had not noticed his arrival. It was surprising that he was in an old overcoat even in this weather. Probably around fifty – fifty-five years of age, he sported an unkempt beard on which were stuck stale food particles from days long gone. He was well-built and looked like he was either an ex-police or army officer. He didn't pay any attention to me and was looking away while he ate the food he had brought. It was something crunchy. And it smelt bad. I wasn't aware of any food item available in Ukraine that made such noise. Annoyed, I looked at the old man. Was there no other place he might have sat?

The old man turned around, as if he had read my mind. He did not stop eating but asked,

'Suicide?'

'Yes.'

'Love?'

I said, 'Yes.' Though that was only half the reason.

But the old man did not turn towards me again. He single-mindedly focused on finishing his food. Then he wiped his hands clean on his overcoat, and walked towards me and sat by my side.

'Are you a refugee?'

'Yes.'

He slid his hand into his bag and drew something out. It was a gun.

'Look, I feel very sorry for you. It has been a week since I shot someone. There is nothing worse than getting hit by a train. Your body will be torn into pieces. You won't even be identified. They will sweep your remains away. In Ukraine, there is no respect for death. Visit Kiev's mortuary. People wait there in long queues to receive the bodies. But in your case, your body won't even remain a body. A gunshot would be perfect. A clean shot in the forehead or a hole in the heart. It will be over in a moment. If you agree, I can shoot you.'

I was now afraid. The old man was looking at the gun lovingly, as if seeing it for the very first time.

'Have you ever shot someone?' he asked.

I answered in the negative.

'Hold this. Man's best invention. Hold this and see how courage flows into you.'

I held the gun. When I pulled the trigger slightly, I felt a strange confidence surge through me. I thought the world was beneath me. I could pull the trigger anytime and kill the old man in front of me. I handed the gun back to him.

'Were you in love with a Russian woman?'

'Her name was Laura. She loved me passionately for about four weeks.'

'Is that the reason?'

'Laura in the movie *Dr Zhivago* was a beautiful woman. This Laura too had the same grey eyes. The same shoulder length blond hair. Lips that shone like the inner side of a conch. She told me that I was her life.'

'Did you love her because she had the name of a character in a romantic film?'

'She would visit me in her Sunday clothes. She was the only bit of happiness in my otherwise pitiable existence. Sometimes I would wait for ten hours, just thinking of her footsteps approaching me.'

'What could you do with her footsteps? Russian women like to keep themselves busy. They like to renew their love every year like they would renew their licences. You want to die now. Go ahead and die. One can die at ten years or at hundred years of age. But what are you leaving behind? Pieces of your body? What have you done for the world to remember you by?

'Man always wallows in his sorrows; he doesn't think of the good things that exist in the world. You want to give up your life for some woman you knew for barely four weeks? How absurd! Is she your world? There is a beautiful thousand-year-old church in the city of Kiev. Have you visited that? The glass chandeliers there weigh four tonnes. You won't see such a marvel anywhere else in the world. They are so beautiful.'

'I'm a refugee. I have no country.'

'A man with no country can fall in love, but he cannot enjoy beauty? You don't need a country to admire a piece of art. You don't need intelligence to be astonished by something. Have you seen the Dnieper river? It runs through three countries to join the Black Sea.'

I did not raise my head to look at the man.

'Come, it's now time for vodka. We cannot spend this beautiful moment in vain.'

His name was Shasha, short for Alexander. We stepped into a bar. The old man ordered a very fine vodka, drunk only by the rich. We had three pegs each. My last ten-dollar note lay crumpled in my pocket. In Ukraine, I could get 1,400,000 coupons for ten dollars. We could spend it drinking vodka for an entire day. But Shasha paid for the vodka and refused to take money from me. I don't remember gulping the fourth peg. I couldn't remember later how I managed to identify my building and reach the eighth floor.

When I woke up the next morning, it took me a moment to realise where I was. I was sleeping on someone else's plastic mat covered in my own vomit. Nauseated I got up hastily, washed my clothes and the mat. I took a bath, wore a lungi and prepared tea. There was no one in the house. They might have gone to see Alex in the hospital. Someone banged on the door very hard. I straightened up. Only the police banged on doors so authoritatively. They normally didn't ring the bell. My heart skipped a beat when I looked through the keyhole. They were dressed in black, wore black boots and carried pistols at the waist. Their caps bore the symbol of a candle between two triangles. They were indeed the police. When one of them opened their mouths to shout, I saw a gold tooth. One in four policemen in Russia had a gold tooth.

Why had they come? Why were they banging on the door? I was confused.

Had they come to check our passports and visas? Perhaps Alex had filed a complaint against me. But Alex's stay was illegal too, how could he lodge a complaint? I thought of something else. Shasha, the old Russian, had handed his gun to me yesterday. I had left my fingerprints on the trigger. Were they here to arrest me for a murder? The answer to all my questions lay on the other side of the door.

SIX

Son of a Chameleon

The policemen rushed into the apartment as soon as I opened the door, strewing the leaves from the soles of their boots across the floor. They ignored me and searched the entire place, including the bathroom and kitchen. They searched through the neatly stacked vessels. They emptied all the boxes and checked my passport and student visa.

Finally, they asked, 'Where is Jayakaran?'

It was then that my heartbeat dropped to normal. They were looking for someone else.

'I don't know. There is nobody by that name here.'

They showed me a photograph of a man who looked like an actor. 'This is Jayakaran. If he comes here, you should inform us,' they said and left as they had come. On his way out, the policeman with the golden tooth saw that my cheek was unmarked and landed a slap.

I was both relieved and surprised. They kept referring to him as Jagayan, but I guessed it must be Jayakaran. The policemen had some information about Jayakaran. Why were they looking for him here? The young man in the photograph must be less than thirty years old and was attractive. It was evident that he was Sri Lankan. What had he done?

Someone hammered on the door again. This time I wasn't worried. I opened the door, and there, before me, stood Jayakaran. In person, he was even more handsome. He was smiling, as if he had won a trophy.

'Is Ravi here?' he asked.

'Brother, aren't you Jayakaran? The police came looking for you.' I couldn't bring myself to tell Jayakaran to leave. Jayakaran's body was taut and muscular, like a tightly wound rope. There was not an extra ounce of flesh on him. He looked attractive when he smiled, his jaws making a triangular shape. I was keen to find out more from him.

'Come in,' I said. Nobody would think of him as a refugee. He wore an expensive coat. His hair was neatly combed and his glance was direct and bold. He walked in without any hesitation and sat cross-legged on a chair that was least damaged. In that moment, I became his slave. If Jayakaran had looked up and said, 'Jump from the eighth floor,' I would have obeyed him.

'Brother, aren't you afraid? The police are looking for you.'

'Ukraine police?' he asked and laughed. 'Where is Ravi?'

'He has stepped out. Why are the police looking for you?'

'You want the story? Get me a beer, and I'll tell you.'

I, the slave, ran and brought the beer can I had saved for myself. I humbly handed it over to Jayakaran. He slipped his right index finger into the pull-tab and yanked it expertly, took a gulp, relaxed, and told me the whole story. I did not interrupt and listened, all ears.

'They caught me at around two a.m. on the border of Greece. I was standing in a spot dented by hundreds of thousands of travellers before me. Because of the dip in the ground, I looked an inch shorter than the others. I have been caught on several occasions, across several countries. But I had never thought I would be caught on that day. My passport and visa were perfect. The cold pierced my long overcoat and I was shivering. The border policeman was looking intently at my visa as if he was analysing an ancient inscription. I was unaware that a passport should have forty-eight pages and that mine had only forty-six. The person who sold it to me had ripped out two pages. I was taken into a small room, which I thought was an elevator. That was the interrogation room.

'"Tell me," said the official seated at a table.

'"What?" I asked, confused.

'"Your story? From the beginning."

'I knew Greek but pretended that I did not. I told them my story in English.

'"Three years ago, in 1983, I joined a ship here in Greece. This ship was called Argo. My first journey was to Brazil. After that I went to many countries. I travelled across the world. Finally, when the ship was sold at Turkey's Bandirma harbour, I lost my job. I didn't know what to do next, but three Pakistani men came to my rescue and changed my life. We stayed in Bosphorus, a beautiful place where the east meets the west. From our hotel, we could see the Blue Mosque. We decided to work for the mafia in Turkey. The mafia functioned like a parallel government there. With their support, I was told that we could tide over any crisis. The Pakistanis taught me everything I needed to know.

'In the 1980s, there was no import of cars in Turkey, and in the black market, prices were exorbitant. If a car was involved in an accident anywhere in Turkey, the mafia would grab its licence plate, import a new car from Switzerland, screw the licence plate on it and sell it. A car could easily fetch 40,000 or 50,000 dollars. Our job was to fly to Switzerland, buy the car they wanted and drive it back to Turkey. It was an easy job. We would start in Zurich, drive through Italy, Yugoslavia, Bulgaria and reach Turkey. We received 5000 dollars for the job. I have even smuggled two cars in a week. Those were the days when I didn't know what to do with that kind of money.

'Once in Switzerland, I fell in love with a woman by just seeing her reflection on a marble floor. She was a swimmer. Her name was Simona. Her eyes were a bright shade of blue. If you looked deep enough into those eyes, you would find yourself in the middle of a sea. I stayed with her whenever I visited Switzerland. I had nothing to worry about in those days. Simona thought I was a rich salesman. One day when I confessed the truth to her, she jumped up and down excitedly. She was adventurous by nature.

'"Take me with you," she said.

'Though I knew that the mafia would not like it, I took a risk and drove 2500 kilometres with her by my side.

'When we reached Turkey, I stopped at the first restaurant we saw. A man outside the restaurant was playing a musical instrument, holding it in both his hands and blowing into it. The instrument sometimes was long, and sometimes got short when he was playing it. I gave him a hundred liras. Simona took my wallet and gave him another hundred. She enjoyed spending my money. When we returned after our meal, there was a car parked in front of ours. There was no one in it, but strange sounds came from its trunk. Simona did not consult me; she took a spanner and broke open the trunk of the car. A huge figure bound hand-and-foot was inside. How could such a large human being be stuffed into a car trunk? He begged us to release him. We had no time to think; we untied him and took him in our car. Simona was excited, like a dog with two tails. She loved adventures.

'The man we had rescued was named Mehmet. He belonged to a different mafia gang. The enemies had kidnapped him and planned to kill him. When we dropped him twenty kilometres later, he was very emotional and said he wouldn't forget us till his last day.

'I handed over the car to my employers, got my money and roamed around with Simona for four days. We stayed in expensive hotels. She took hundreds of pictures of the Ayasofya, a 1500-year-old church which had first been converted into a mosque and later a museum. She asked me to pose in front of it for a photo.

'"Smile," she said. "Smile, no? Am I a dentist or an income tax official?" she asked.

'"Who is an income tax official?" I had no idea that there existed someone like that and that people had to pay taxes on their income to them.

'That night was unforgettable. Simona slipped off her footwear, and it was odd when she lay between me and the wall. She would sleep with her legs open but entwined at the feet, like that of a crocodile. She had seen several paintings at the museum and she had a question. "How come leaves in the creeper bend and twist in such a way as to hide 'those' parts in all the paintings of Adam and Eve?" I explained the reason with my tongue inside her mouth. Her eye makeup was shining like fish scales. I kissed her on the back of her head where the hair changed colour. I could hear her breath. She could hear mine. We did not sleep that night. Neither of us knew that it would be our last night together. I did not meet her after that night.

'From across the departure gate in the airport, she raised her hands as if making a pledge and bade goodbye. As the escalator descended, she disappeared little by little.

'When I was returning from the airport, two people followed me. The Turkish police. They asked for my passport. I realised what the issue was. When entering Turkey, they would stamp the picture of a car. The stamp would be removed when the car left the country. "Where is the car?" the cop asked me. I was silent. Soon I was thrown into a jail with forty others. The mafia rescued me from that hellish place. Since the police were now suspicious of me, I was of no use to the mafia. But they were decent enough to buy me a ticket to Qatar and find me a job on a ship there.

'There were nineteen people including me who boarded the ship in Qatar for work. We introduced ourselves. Nobody laughed when I said my name and that was some solace. The ship was very old and looked haunted. At about 11 p.m., the captain and two officials boarded the ship. There was nothing on the ship. Not enough food either. Nobody knew where the ship was headed. We spoke to each other surreptitiously and in fear. We sensed that a grave danger was imminent. On the fourth day, the ship docked at Djibouti. No goods were loaded. When we crossed the Eden harbour in a few days, we were even more worried. A Christian fellow working with me started crying.

'"You need no talent for crying," I told him. "Even a child can cry. We need to work as sailors now."

'He was trembling as he made the sign of the cross. I asked him why. He pointed to the grave of the first human being to die on this earth.

'"Adam's grave?" I asked.

'"No, Adam was the first human being. But Abel, Adam's second son, was the first one to die. He was murdered. Make a sign of the cross, you will be blessed," he said, and I made the sign.

'The last meal we had had been two days ago. From the previous day, there had been no water either. It was ten at night. The ship started shuddering, and I knew the ship could not survive at this speed. Just when I thought nothing worse could happen, something did! The ship crashed against a rock. In that moment, a calendar turned upside down, and I could see some writing in a child's hand.

'"Danger! They have a plan to wreck this ship and claim insurance! Escape immediately!"

'When I went to the upper deck, people were escaping in lifeboats. I too jumped into one, and they took us to Cairo, gave us tickets and salaries, and asked us to go back to our countries. All my eighteen colleagues accepted the offer. I figured out their plan. They would break the ship down and earn millions. We were no longer useful to them. They gave me a ticket to go home.

'These tickets were booked on the 14th, but the accident happened on the 17th—how was this possible? "This is a conspiracy. I am going to communicate this to the Lloyds Insurance Company. All of us need compensation," I said.

'"We will take you to our boss," they said.

'Two days passed. They took me through many bylanes and alleys of Cairo and finally to the basement of an old house. Two guards stood clutching their rifles. The leader was seated on a lion-shaped chair, with half his body protruding outside it. He was bare-chested and sat wearing a lungi, his stomach folded up on itself. He turned to face me and I screamed, "Mehmet!" It was the man who had been dumped in the trunk of a car. He stood up with some difficulty and came towards me crying, "My friend!"

'"I have orders to eliminate you. You saved me once, and so, I am now saving you. And I will give you anything you ask for. But if I catch you the next time, I will have to kill you," he said.

'I could have asked for an American or French visa. Or even a visa to Simona's country. But I asked to be sent to Greece. He gave me enough money and helped me reach here.

'The two policemen at the border looked at me in utter disbelief. "Why did you come here again, you idiot?" one of them asked.

'"This is where I started, my friend," I said.

'Now a third person arrived. He appeared to be their superior and looked at me as if he was appraising a weird creature.

'"What does he say? This son of a chameleon?" he asked.

'"He is spinning stories," the other two policemen told him. Then the three of them discussed something and fought loudly. They could imprison me, but they would incur a loss. If they sent me back, the government would have to pay for my tickets. A greater loss. The third official held up page number forty-six of my passport and said in Greek, "He must be having a lot of money, why can't we kill him?"

'The men whose legacy was that of Pythagoras, Archimedes and Plato used their tiny brains to decide what to do with me. They had heated arguments about me. But I was laughing. It was three years, four months and eight days since I had left Sri Lanka. They might think of any punishment, but it wouldn't come anywhere close to what I had already suffered. I was fine with any decision they made. Unfortunately, they had only one country; I had countries all over the world. But look, I am here. The police are looking out for me.'

The story was over. The beer was over too. Jayakaran stood up. He appeared taller than when he first came in. He did not look like someone the police were hunting for. The details of his crimes were mind-boggling.

'Ask Ravi to contact me immediately,' he said.

'All right, brother, but where should I ask him to meet you?'

'He knows.' Jayakaran smiled. 'What's your name?'

My happiness was indescribable. I said, 'Nishant', as if I was speaking a word that hadn't been used in a long time. For I was travelling under a false name, 'Ramesh'.

'Oh, good,' he said, and opened the door. He went down the steps without waiting for the elevator. He appeared smaller as he walked down. Now only his shoulders were visible and finally, his head. Then he disappeared fully. I felt depressed, as if I had lost something precious. I sat down on the same chair Jayakaran had occupied a minute ago.

SEVEN

I Read but Once

Whenever I climbed a tree, my mother would shout from below, 'Careful, son. You might fall.'

Ahalya wasn't the same. 'Careful, gravity, careful,' she would say. She thought differently. I took a liking to her.

I liked houses that had windows facing roads. I could spend any number of hours watching the road. I remembered what Ambikapathi master had told me. 'The right woman for you has already taken birth somewhere. She is waiting for you. All you have to do is find her.'

I had stopped looking for her long ago. A man deserves only two failures in love. I was firm that I did not need a third one. I continued in this manner, standing on the eighth floor, looking at the roads. I could see the agent approaching the apartment building. A young woman was walking beside him. A new refugee. Her face wasn't clear from that distance. Her hair was loose. The way she walked and the way she held onto her handbag left me unsettled. My heart began to beat rapidly. I wasn't sure what this was. My mouth uttered a prayer. Who could she be? If she was a refugee, there would be one more person amongst us. But she was alone. How long would she be around and where was she headed?

The name of the new refugee was Ahalya. The agent introduced her to everyone. She was headed to Germany, where her brother was already a refugee. She must be seventeen or eighteen. She did not seem new to Ukraine. This new country did not daunt her. She had the confidence and poise of someone who had spent a decade here. She had been selected for a medical course in Sri Lanka but had left it behind to go to Germany. She would stay in Ukraine for some time before finding her way to Germany. I was afraid of looking into her eyes. Her intellect shone in them.

Till we retired to bed, I couldn't speak a word to her. Eswaranathan assumed the responsibility of being at her beck and call. It was a disgusting sight. His wife's eyes were piercing him with rage. Forty-year-old Eswaranathan thus put an invisible fence around Ahalya. For how long, I asked myself.

The next morning too, the leech-like Eswaranathan did not leave Ahalya alone. But something else happened. Ahalya walked towards me and sought my help. My jaw dropped at this. And I could see Eswaranathan burning with envy. 'What is it?' I asked, managing to speak coherently. I was surprised that she chose me, out of everyone there. The reason was soon evident. 'You have stayed here longer than the others, the agent said you speak a bit of Russian too, and that you are familiar with places here. I need to buy some stuff. Could we do some shopping?'

I couldn't believe my luck. What else could this opportunity to spend some hours with her be if not the handiwork of God?

When we started shopping together, she walked very close to me. I thought she would buy winter footwear, thermal wear or gloves. I was amused when she told me what she intended to buy. She wanted to buy a Roman-numeral wristwatch. I knew they were not available in Ukraine. People were after normal watches. But we would have to return immediately if I told her that. I was keen to prolong our time together, so we went to many stores. I asked her why she specifically wanted a Roman-numeral watch. Her answer was even more amusing.

She had learnt by rote the names of several kings when reading history. She was fascinated by names like King Henry VIII, Richard III, Louis XIV, etc. It would have been nice to have such numbers suffixed to her name too—Ahalya III, Ahalya VI, Ahalya XIV and so on. But the Roman numerals were reserved for kings. She eventually decided that at least her watch would have Roman numerals. She was upset when she couldn't find such a watch in Sri Lanka, but she was hopeful that in Ukraine she would find one. Ukraine too shattered her hopes.

Over the next few days, I spoke to her about the watch. I told her I had a friend in Moscow who could help get what she wanted. It helped boost my chances of a conversation with her. One day I mentioned a random shop to her and took her there, spending three hours with her as a result. But we couldn't find the watch.

'Is this all there is to your lives?' she asked one day. 'Some of you sleep through the day. Some watch TV. Look at Premachandran—all he does is drink and sleep. He is of no use, like a milestone with no marks on it. Look at Vairavanathan—

he has grown waist-length hair. He spends the entire day playing cards. How can they waste their time this way?'

'We are refugees, what else can we do? We have to wait, not knowing what plans the agent has for us.'

'Is this a reason? Shame,' she said.

Then I told her about the house owner on the ninth floor, who had offered to teach us Russian for free. We decided to go together. Much later, I would regret suggesting it.

Within two minutes of introducing the landlady to Ahalya, I became a stranger. It was incredible. Ahalya would often tell me that she remembered things she had read or heard only once. On that day, I was to witness it. We learnt Russian for an hour on that day. Ahalya learnt every word by rote. When returning, it became clear to me that she had learned more Russian in an hour than I had in a year. Ahalya was happy about it. I felt stupid standing beside her. But I was happy too.

One afternoon, when we went to meet the landlady, she was reading. When asked, she said she was reading Chekhov. 'He is the master of short fiction,' she said. 'He changed its format completely. Most stories have no beginning nor an end. The reader has to complete them.'

'Let's skip the lesson today, tell us the story you are reading instead,' Ahalya told her.

A well-built but lazy guard was working in a garden. His name was Savka. There was something fascinating about him. Women came looking for him. The man who handled the railway signal and his wife lived a few metres away from the garden. The wife's name was Agafya. One day she came looking for the guard. She had brought food with her. 'My husband has gone to handle the signals. I should go back before he returns,' she said. But the guard didn't pay any attention to her.

His hobby was to catch nightingales with his bare hands. He loved the challenge it posed. He relished the pies and mashed potato Agafya had brought him. She kept reminding him of her husband who would come back after the train left. He took his time to eat the food. Just then, a nightingale sang. 'I will be right back,' he told her, and disappeared to catch it. He could hear the sound of the train leaving. Agafya decided to leave for her home but couldn't bring herself to do it. Her husband would be back within moments. When she decided to wait for just a minute longer, Savka came back. On seeing him, she decided to take the risk and spend the night with him. If their relationship was exposed, he would be lashed publicly in the village court and her husband would abandon her.

The next day, her husband stood outside Savka's door and called her—'Agafya, Agafya!' She left and walked towards her husband. He stood motionless. On seeing him, she was gripped by a sense of fear. Still, she walked towards him.

This was the story.

We were silent while returning home. Suddenly, Ahalya recited a poem to me: *'Siru kottu perum pazham thoongiyaangu/ ival uyir thava siruthu, kaamamo perithe'*.

Shocked, I asked her, 'This sounds like Tamil, what does it mean?'

'*Kurunthogai*—like the big jackfruit that hangs on a slender bough, her love for you is big, but her life is very short.'

'How do you know all this?'

'I need to read but once. I never forget.'

It was her birthday. I ran here and there and found a Roman-numeral wristwatch for her. Everything was fine that morning. There were puddles of water on the streets after some rains. As if the sun was anxious to disappear, night fell all of a sudden. We stood outside. When we looked at the sky and then the land, the scene was mysteriously beautiful. The stars were shining in the rainwater. It looked as though they could be caught with bare hands. The stars moved when the water stirred. Standing in the midst of it, I presented the watch to her. She was overwhelmed. She was shining bright, her large eyes glowed. I stood not knowing what to do next, like a warrior who had lost his weapon. She couldn't contain herself. She drew my head towards her and kissed me. I felt like I was floating among the stars. It was incredible that I, born in Kuppilan, and she, in Uduvil, were meeting in a hamlet called Trishna in Ukraine in the midst of this galaxy of stars. Everything was intoxicating.

'We shouldn't forget this day,' she said, speaking my mind. 'Look at the stars in the water. It is the Orion constellation. In Tamil, it is called Mirugaseeridam, a man hunting a pack of deer. The four big stars are hounds. The smaller stars are deer. The one in their midst is the hunter. They are our witnesses.'

'How do you know all this?' I asked her.

'It's in the Rig Veda.'

'Oh, yes. You only read once but never forget,' I said, removing my hands from her pockets and hugging her close.

EIGHT

Canada is Doing Nothing

One morning, I woke up and started making a list of things I liked about Ahalya.

Eyes larger than her face

Wearing socks

Bending down to pick up something

Standing on her toes to fetch an item

Sitting cross-legged

Wearing an overcoat and tucking her hands into its pockets

Pushing her hair back by tossing her head

Smiling with eyes closed

The trembling upper lip when angry

The way she says that she has got it as a loan from God

Claiming to be faster than a comet

When saying goodbye, gesturing as if signalling not to take a photo

Ahalya came up behind me, stealthily, when I was making the list. I tried to hide it, but she went after me. She managed to wrest the paper from me, read it and started laughing uproariously.

'What is this—loan from God?'

'I once asked how your eyes were so beautiful, and that was your response,' I reminded her.

'And what about wearing socks?'

'When you are wearing socks, your entire body bends over, reaches down and concentrates on your heel point. Your foot slowly disappears into the socks. It is so exciting to watch.'

'What makes me ugly? Make a list of that too,'

'I tried but couldn't come up with anything.'

'How is that possible? Beauty and ugliness coexist.'

'Is that a universal truth?'

'I have read how love that ran like heavy floods in the river dried up to become sand. Let's talk about Chekhov's Agafya. What do you think of her? Was she right?' Ahalya asked.

'What is right and what is wrong? Who am I to judge? More importantly, I don't know the entire story. It has neither a proper beginning nor a proper ending.'

'Women are always this way. They ponder over their decisions only after they are taken. Agafya ruined her life for a few moments of lust. Did she regret it later? The readers have no idea.'

'It keeps the world moving—looking for something that doesn't exist.'

Once I made the remark, we started thinking about it. We were evidently sunk in our own thoughts.

I did not start the fight, and many were witness to it. Around lunch time, things started in an unexpected way. I was in charge of cooking and, as usual, the lunch menu was rotis, dhal and boiled eggs. Eggs were a regular feature of our meals as they were cheap. I had made fried eggs for Ahalya since she did not eat boiled eggs. Everybody served themselves and moved away. Then Ahalya served herself the fried eggs. It was at that point that Vairavanathan started off, as if waiting for the right opportunity.

Vairavanathan was slender but firm and had long hair. It always looked like his lungi would fall off any moment. His skin was pale where the shirt covered it and dark where exposed. Seated on the floor, he would play cards with a group. You could always see him holding a card over his head, wondering if he should throw it down or not.

Ever since Ahalya arrived, he had been eyeing her, but could not pluck up the courage to speak to her. He wouldn't look her in the eye. He would either look down or away. But he made his burning desire evident. He watched from the corner of his eye as Ahalya left with her plate of fried eggs. When angered, Vairavanathan's face flushed as if he had the measles. Covering his ear with his left hand and extending his right arm, he sang a popular song in a dramatic style.

'Along with the soup of wingless chicken,
I also need fried eggs and a whole duck.'

'Wait—what?' I screamed and rushed holding the plate over my head. Eswaranathan did a sensible thing that day. He intervened and blocked me. He dragged me aside and said, 'Vairavanathan is like a dog chained to a tree. He'll keep running around the tree. And when the chain hurts, he'll stop. You carry on with your work.'

And so, the first battle was contained before it started. I thought of it as an arrow that had just missed me.

The second incident too started with a song. Ahalya always wore jeans and T- shirt. On that day, she wore a red salwar and sported a red bindi as if she was going out. When I saw her, I was afraid that my heart would split into two. Ahalya was now adept at grasping what my eyes said. Vairavanathan started singing an old song, *'Mella nada, mella nada meniennagum'* (walk slowly, slowly my dear, lest your tender body gets hurt).

Pushing my chair back, I rose and screamed, *'Meni punnaagum!'* (you'll get badly hurt!) and hit him. Others immediately rushed in and caught me. These feuds could not be settled by the agent.

'Are you school boys? Am I your class teacher? You will have to sort out these issues yourselves. Else I will send you all back home,' he would say.

Ahalya did not speak to me for the rest of the day. Her lips were closed, but her eyes were speaking to me. Finally, we met in the kitchen at night when no one was around. She hugged me passionately, as if I had rescued her from a prison. 'Hold me tight, this is not enough. Hold me like you'd hold a bow before letting an arrow go,' she said.

'Are we in ancient times?' I asked. 'To hold you like Rama held the bow? Shall I hold you like a gun?'

'Idiot, this is from an old poem—*'Villagaviralinporunthi'*—holding the lover tight like a bow.'

'Where did you get this from? Oh right! You read once and never forget.'

For the next few moments, both of us were in a state of excitement—like getting drenched in a mild rain.

When I started to talk, Ahalya placed a finger on my mouth and stopped me. Then she planted a kiss on my lips.

'What are you doing?' I asked in panic.

'I'm measuring your lips,' she responded nonchalantly. In a tender voice I said, 'Like Vairavanathan, I also want wingless chicken soup, fried eggs and a whole duck, woman!'

She laughed and pushed me away.

I stood in the same place.

I now had a new cause for worry. I was afraid that the agent might bring some bad news anytime. After Ahalya's arrival, I stopped being fond of travelling. What if the agent sent her and me with different groups? Nobody could decipher how his mind worked. He would send someone off all alone, and then a group of refugees would follow. It was difficult to predict. Yesurasa, who turned his head from side to side like a horse, was sent off alone three days ago and he had already reached London. I asked Ahalya what we would do in case the agent decided to send us separately.

'We'll reject it if the agent comes up with such a thoughtless plan. We will tell him we want to travel together,' she said.

'You have to go to Germany. Your brother lives there. I'm headed to Canada. How will our travelling together be possible?' I asked her.

'Why are you going to Canada?'

'Why? Because Canada is sitting and doing nothing. It is the second largest country in the world. The country is expecting my arrival.'

She laughed. 'You will be a refugee in Canada. And I will be one in Germany. Let one of us get permanent residence in either of the countries. We can work this out later. We should create our own future. We cannot expect anyone else to create it for us.'

'You have a brother waiting in Germany. Whom do I have there?'

'Don't you have me? Isn't that enough? A scientist once said that the number of humans who were born and died on this earth since its origin is smaller than the number of humans living on earth today. The world population today is approximately 5.7 billion. There are so many human beings on earth today. Everyone has a life to live. Wouldn't we have one too?'

That sounded fair enough.

The agent was a very cautious person. The kind who checks the expiry date on the bottle of poison before consuming it. I was alarmed when he arrived early in the morning. He looked at both sides of the room, as if he were crossing a road but did not utter a word, making me tense. Why was he hesitating?

'A route is open now; four people could go. The border guards have been bribed. But the group has to leave immediately. It is your responsibility to behave in a way that will not arouse any suspicion. You will board a train to Slovakia. There would be rigorous surveillance at Mukachevo station. If you manage to dodge that, it's possible to reach Germany without a hitch after that.'

It was decided that Eswaranathan, his wife, Ahalya and I would leave. Vairavanathan arrived from somewhere, gripping his hair with both his hands, and demanded that he too be sent along. The agent snapped at him, saying he knew when to send and whom to send. Vairavanathan was furious but could do nothing. Ahalya wasn't aware of any of this. She lay sleeping, face down, but woke up on hearing the agent's voice. She had a problem. The 400 dollars that her brother had promised to send hadn't reached her. She gave the 100 dollars she had saved for her watch to the agent and promised to send the rest after reaching Germany. But the agent would have none of it. Without hesitating for a moment, I handed over the 300 dollars I had. Ahalya did not thank me; instead, she gave me a look that only I understood.

On the train journey, Ahalya opened up for the first time about her mother who had worked for a merciless small-time trader. She would leave for work crying and would come back crying even harder. She wouldn't raise her voice. She only knew how to love. 'As a child, I would try and imagine the many ways to keep my mother happy. One day, I was sitting on the floor studying. Amma swept the room with a broom around me. She thought my studies would be disturbed if she asked me to move. Every time I think of her, I only see the image of her holding a broom. I was in school at the time. Early one morning, Amma combed my hair with a broken comb. When she stroked my hair, I thought she had never done that before. She left home, but never came back. Even today, I don't know if she's alive or not.'

Eswaranathan bought lunch for us—bread and bananas. He smiled broadly when he said that our next meal would be in Slovakia. It could be in a jail in Ukraine too, I said. A young Russian couple travelled with us. The woman was eating something without removing her gloves. The smell of cheese triggered our hunger. When the Russian lady said something, it took Ahalya a moment to realise that she was speaking in English. Ahalya responded to her in Russian. The couple were travelling with their six-year-old son and two-year-old daughter. Unaware that it no longer meant anything, throughout the journey, the son held a Russian flag: the red flag with sickle and hammer. The cheeks of the baby girl were red as an apple. Ahalya picked her up and caressed the child. She had never seen someone so fair and pretty. She asked something and the child responded.

Mukachevo station was busy. The border police entered the compartments. Their height, grey uniforms, boots and voices triggered panic. Their faces were bloated and shining. I had never seen such faces before. I asked Ahalya to hand over the baby to the parents. Instead, she hugged the child even closer. The police spoke to the Russian family first and they responded. They asked the same question to Ahalya and she responded in Russian. Eswaranathan blurted out something. He and his wife were made to get off the train. I wasn't breathing evenly. My heart was thudding. The police didn't ask me a single question; they just hit me on the back of my head and dragged me by the collar to the platform. I couldn't utter a single word in Russian, learning which I had spent three years. The words remained locked in my throat.

About twenty people were removed from the train. Shocked, I kept watching Ahalya. But she wasn't looking at me. I shouted her name when the train started to move. She never turned to look at me. She was engaged in an animated conversation with the Russian couple. The police beat me as I yelled her name over and over again. They thought that I was protesting in my language. Those of us who were left behind were imprisoned for four days and questioned. We were beaten up and our money was taken away. We were sometimes served unsweetened tea. The next meal didn't happen in Slovakia as Eswaranathan had prophesied. When we returned to the eighth floor apartment, the agent complained about how the border guard had cheated him after taking our money. No one offered us any comfort. On the contrary, the agent expected us to console him. 'It is difficult now. All routes are closed,' he said. I thought he was looking for some more money. It turned out to be true.

A week later, the agent informed us that Ahalya had reached Germany. I expected a phone call from her, which never came. I expected a long letter from her, which too never came. The agony of those three months can't be described.

'Why did she do that? Was it planned? Didn't she hold my hands with the Orion constellation as witness? Didn't she say she would reach me faster than a comet? Did she forget me at the same speed?'

One day, the agent came to me, smiling. I thought he had brought some news of her. I asked if there was any news for me. The agent said, 'She has sent your money back through someone, asking that it be given to you. She did not forget the help you gave her in an emergency. A very honest person.'

So saying, he handed over 300 dollars to me.

'Isn't there a letter?' I asked the agent again. He shook his head in the negative. I realised that Ahalya hadn't just returned my money but had settled all accounts with me.

I thought of the days in which we had learnt Russian together on the ninth floor. It had been a very happy period in my life. I was obsessed with her. How many times would she have said that she never forgot anything.

Had she forgotten how we had loved each other? How easily she forgot me! Wouldn't she think of me even when she looked at the roman-numeral watch on her wrist?

When the pain got too much to bear, I would call her name out to myself—Ahalya! Ahalya!

It sometimes sounded like Agafya! Agafya!

NINE

High-Caste Pushpanathan

Never in my whole life will I forget the day I witnessed a murder in broad daylight, from a distance of ten feet. It was on 9 April 1996.

While setting off from Sri Lanka, I could not have imagined that such things would happen in my life. Two people were fighting for a very trivial reason. The competition was about who would be the first to reach the peak of stupidity. From that day on, I felt I had to exit that place as soon as possible because I realised I was becoming and behaving like those around me.

It took me three months to recover from Ahalya's departure. When alone, I would convert my pain into words, poems. Yet, the pain remained. While in Ukraine, every single day she would ask me the time of sunrise. What would she do with that piece of information? I never found out. She was mysterious. It would have been some consolation if she had written to me. Had it all been a drama? Why? I couldn't get over the betrayal. She had mentioned the *Kurunthogai,* the *Rig Veda* and the Orion constellation. Then the woman, who remembered everything, forgot me.

A new agent called Madhorupaagan was now in charge of us. I was by now used to agents changing often. The new agent said we would have to look for another place since a new group of refugees was on the way. 'We need a separate house with two rooms. An apartment is not good enough.'

But nothing happened. There were many telephone calls. The agent had contacts everywhere. He received calls from America, Canada, Europe, Australia, India and Sri Lanka. He would have long conversations with those who called. There was no control mechanism in place for calls. Inspired by this, the refugees too made phone calls. The agent didn't mind.

One night, at around ten o'clock, when everyone was getting ready to go to bed, Madhorupaagan rushed in and asked us to prepare to leave. 'Where to?' we asked. His only response was, 'Get ready now!' We started packing bags and suitcases. The clothes that were still damp from washing were also dumped into our bags. Someone put all the kitchen utensils in a box. Everything was wrapped up in minutes.

As we queued up on the road, Madhorupaagan walked behind us. There was a vehicle waiting a short distance away. It carried us to an independent house rented by Madhorupaagan. I had been sceptical until now. I thought it was unfair to not have informed the landlady about the move. I asked Madhorupaagan about this in private. He spoke as if uttering a secret onstage.

'We ran up a two-thousand-dollar telephone bill. It was wise to run away before she asked us to pay.'

I was repulsed by this reply. Could anyone be such a cheat? I recalled the happy days I had spent learning Russian from the landlady. I recalled the twelve-course meal she had sent on Christmas day and how Chandra mami had relished it. I felt totally dejected recalling her stories and the Troika dance. The rent was her source of livelihood. I felt ashamed at the kind of men I was associating with. I could do nothing but mutter that it was a 'betrayal'.

The new place was an old house in a corner of a street. The trees, shrubs and grass there reminded me of my village. Since a building was coming up nearby, the noise of construction labourers filled the air in the day. In the night, we could hear the sounds of the night birds. One or two labourers would wear reflective gear and guard the building, speaking in a foreign language. The old apartment had been like a prison. In a scenic neighbourhood like this, it was possible to breathe freely. A tributary of the Dnieper river flowed nearby, its sound soothing. How happy Ahalya would have been in this place! I was reminded of the kiss I had planted on her warm neck after loosening her sweater. I chased the memory away.

Madhorupaagan brought six additional refugees to the new house. Our total count now stood at fourteen. Among the new entrants was a person called Keyar. He wasn't a refugee but an assistant to the agent. The rest did not look like refugees. They looked rough and carefree, and behaved as if they had lived in Russia all their lives. There were also a three-year-old child and its mother, who looked about forty. What was surprising was how Madhorupaagan had assembled this unusual group.

Within twelve hours of their landing, a man named Pushpanathan appointed himself as the leader of the group. The rest spoke in hushed tones about how affluently he had lived in Saudi Arabia. He could invite danger anytime. He was an old-time football player and walked about as arrogantly as an emperor. Even Madhorupaagan was respectful towards him.

Pushpanathan would lie down on his back and smoke Marlboro cigarettes endlessly, as if to fill up the ashtray placed on his stomach as speedily as possible.

Russian Bear was the cheapest brand of beer available locally; it gave the drinker an instant high. No day of Pushpanathan's was complete without it. He once told me, 'I'm a *Veera Saiva Vellalar*.'

'What does that mean?' I asked in all innocence.

'You idiot, I belong to the highest caste. You should inquire about my reputation in my village. When I walk on the road, no one dares to cross my path.'

Two women did all the cooking in the new house. They had left behind their native homes but not the chore of cooking. One of them was just like Chandra mami. The other was the 'comb mami'; she always had a comb stuck in her hair, as a sign of either waiting to comb her hair or of having just completed the task. It was Keyar who decided what was to be cooked each day. He would shop for groceries, always carrying a pencil to jot down the expenses.

High-caste Pushpanathan was a glutton. He needed different kinds of meat cooked in different styles every day. He hated Keyar and accused him of cheating by buying cheap stuff despite the agent giving him good money. Keyar did not talk much. But when Pushpanathan finished his long list of accusations, Keyar would tease him with a choice remark. Pushpanathan would start all over again and not stop until he ran out of beer or cuss words.

One day, high-caste Pushpanathan rode to the market on a cycle to buy quality stuff for cooking. Keyar let him go on his behalf. The cycle was to be chain-locked to a tree. On that day, Pushpanathan couldn't find a tree to chain his cycle to. There was another locked cycle nearby. Pushpanathan chained his cycle to it and went to the market. When he returned, a young Russian woman wearing a yellow necklace and a matching coat was shouting at him in Russian. He was first astonished by the kind of deafening sounds that came from the throat of such a young girl. He responded to her in broken English. She couldn't understand him and he couldn't understand her. Then it struck Pushpanathan—why should he respond to her in English? He picked the best cuss words in Tamil and hurled them at her.

When he left on his cycle without ending the fight, the young woman followed him. Words kept tumbling out of her mouth as if they wanted to be free. Pushpanathan wouldn't have encountered such an adversary in all his life; he reached our building and rushed into the house. The construction labourers standing around nodded in agreement upon hearing her side of the story. I saw that things were getting out of hand. I apologised to her in Russian. I had some cheese from a dollar store, which is hard to get in Russia. It could be bought only by paying in dollars. I gave her the cheese to buy peace, and her tirade stopped abruptly. In an instant, her expression changed from anger to smiles. When she left on her cycle, Pushpanathan, who was in hiding till then, emerged and screamed, 'Tell that whore that I am a Veera Saiva Vellalar.'

After this incident, Keyar resumed the responsibility of buying groceries. One day, Keyar left for the market in his usual brown coat only to rush back. He said that there was shellfish in a bend in the Dnieper river. Pushpanathan was the first to leap towards the river. Throughout the day, we caught shellfish. In summer, shellfish would be stuck to the rocks in large numbers. Pushpanathan was very fond of shellfish, and for the next ten days, there was shellfish in all three meals. Led by Pushpanathan, we would stand in the river, knee-deep, every day, and gather shellfish. The two women in charge of the kitchen would remove the flesh from the shell and make different dishes. They made curry one day, and sautéed it on the next. On another day, they fried the shellfish. When they cooked it along with eggplants, as demanded by Pushpanathan, it tasted heavenly, and he devoured half of it. There was only one small problem during these times. Cooked shellfish turned blue. Those who ate it also had their lips turn blue. The women suffered more. No lipstick of any kind could cover the blue tint on their lips. For about a week, we all sported blue lips.

One day, the two cooks were boiling the shellfish. When the mouths of the shellfish opened, they sliced the flesh and put it in a pan. When watching this, I was reminded again of Ahalya. I was filled with her thoughts. My heart pounded and my body heated up. I hadn't thought of her for several weeks. I asked myself, 'Why should you think of someone who rejected you?' But I was confused and wanted to speak to her. I begged the agent, but the agent said he didn't have her number. I roamed about, as if possessed. I could forget her only when another big problem showed up.

The reason for remembering her again was a fish lying in the centre of the table with eyes wide open. An agent from France had brought some Tamil video cassettes. Those were days of celebration. From morning to night, we would watch the cassettes over and over again.

On that day, we were watching *Thottachinungi*, a movie featuring Raghuvaran, Revathi and Karthik. Every magazine had praised the movie. Several people had recommended it in letters and over the telephone.

Everyone sat together and watched the movie. When the women and men were singing the praises of Raghuvaran's histrionics, Death had begun its slow but sure journey towards our house. When the movie was played for the second time, Keyar left for the market. When he came back, Pushpanathan, who was watching the movie, rushed to the kitchen. His intent was to find out what Keyar had bought. Keyar had bought gulbya fish. It was a cheap variety that shone like a star fish and tasted like water. It was a suitable fish to smoke or to use for pickling. Pushpanathan was fond of the expensive mackerel. The sounds of a fight reverberated in the kitchen.

'You are swindling money by buying cheap fish.'

Keyar's head rotated like a turtle's. It was difficult to comprehend whether he was agreeing with or refuting the accusation.

'Do you think this is a restaurant? This is all we refugees can afford,' Keyar screamed, raising his pencil.

The fight continued. 'You have revealed your low-caste mentality,' Pushpanathan lashed out.

'You will come around if you are thrown into jail here, like you were in Saudi Arabia,' said Keyar.

Those were Keyar's last words.

Pushpanathan picked up the fish-knife and stabbed Keyar. Those who were watching the movie stopped it and rushed towards them.

On checking if Keyar was dead, Pushpanathan began to tremble. The women started wailing. On hearing the news, Madhorupaagan moved at the speed of light. If the police came, they would beat up everyone and deport us. Madhorupaagan retained three courageous men with him and sent the rest to another agent's place. He decided to concoct a story about Russian robbers breaking in and killing Keyar. But the police arrived, informed by those working in the next building. They handcuffed everyone, wrapped our faces in black plastic covers and took us in a vehicle. There was no enquiry. All of us were beaten up. I told them in Russian that Pushpanathan was the murderer and he admitted to his crime. The police registered the crime but continued to beat the others.

'You have caught the criminal, why are you still beating us?' I asked.

'You are right,' they said and released us.

The police arrested the murderer immediately but removed the body much later. Even in death, Keyar was holding a pencil. His brown overcoat was hanging from a chair. The three-year-old child who had never seen blood saw him and said that 'a red worm was coming out of his nose'. The child didn't even know the Tamil word for it.

The house did not appear like a place where a murder had just taken place or where a corpse had lain on the floor. We dressed each other's wounds caused by the police and went back to watching the movie.

The way Raghuvaran walked and spoke, the way he brushed his hair back with his hands—everything reminded us of Pushpanathan. We thought of how he would stuff shellfish into his mouth. In the night, the two women cooked the fish that had led to the fight. They also made wheat puttu. Everyone was hungry. We relished the meal; it tasted really good. Neither the person who bought the fish nor the person who had fought for it was around to taste it. That day—9 April 1996—ended like any other.

I felt sad thinking of how I was caught amongst murderers, lazy men and drunkards. After a long gap, I called Ambikapathi master and shared my woes. He said, 'There's nothing new about this Nishant. Everyone around you is good. One could be poor; the other might be uneducated; the third person might not be famous. They might be without friends or relatives. But it is entirely different and torturous to be without a country. It is the worst form of punishment. They were not born that way. They were not that way when they left Sri Lanka. Circumstances transformed them. Don't stop helping them. A candle that lights another loses nothing. But try and leave the place soon. Or you too might end up like them.'

I found the agent from France helpful in one respect. He had brought blank student visa cards. I trained myself in preparing student visas. For every student visa, I earned ten dollars. I made five to six fake student visas every week and sold them. Like Sri Lankan students, those from Afghanistan and Kurdistan also required them. Some weeks, I made ten visas. In weeks like those, I forgot that I was a refugee waiting to go to another country.

One day, I left to see the old apartment without informing the agent. A new tenant had occupied the eighth floor. I went to the ninth floor and rang the bell. The landlady opened the door, hugged me and wept. It was hard to see an old woman cry openly. I apologised to her over and over again. She couldn't comprehend half of what I said. I gave her 200 dollars that I had earned from selling forged visas and said that the agent would give her the remaining money. I promised to pay her if he didn't. When I left, I thought I would never forgive Madhorupaagan for cheating that good soul.

Pushpanathan's case dragged on for almost eight months. His argument was that the murder happened in defence. Keyar had assaulted him and he struck him in self-defence. The judge sentenced him to seven years of rigorous imprisonment. Pushpanathan had thought he would go scott-free. For some time, he stood still, mouth agape. To undergo imprisonment in a foreign country was agonising. At that moment, he would have certainly thought of his parents. He hung his head and stood, thinking of something.

The twelve-page judgement was in Russian. It would be valid only when Pushpanathan read it, understood it thoroughly and signed it. A woman translator translated it from Russian to English, and I translated it from English to Tamil and secured Pushpanathan's signature. He held aloft the ink pen, thought deeply and finally signed his name—Kathiravelu Pushpanathan. I felt bad for him.

In the eight-month duration of the case, high-caste Pushpanathan changed a lot. He lost weight and grew skeletal. I was his only visitor. He was surrounded by many prisoners. If he sneezed, his elbows would hit four others. To whom would he complain about the food in jail? Pushpanathan showed me the photograph of a smiling three-year-old girl..

'Who's this?'

'My daughter.'

I was astonished. He had never spoken about her. On a crumpled paper, he wrote something and handed it to me. It had a Saudi Arabia address.

'This is my daughter's address. Do me a favour. She is fond of Kitkat chocolates. Could you buy some from the dollar store and send it to her?'

'Are chocolates not available in Saudi Arabia?'

'Oh lots! But she'll be happy to receive a parcel from her father. She'll jump for joy.'

'When was this photograph taken?'

'Twenty years ago.'

Madhorupaagan didn't visit Pushpanathan even once.

What happened to Pushpanathan after that? Was he ever released? Was he alive? What was he doing now? He was perhaps the last high-caste Veera Saiva Vellalar born in Jaffna, deported from Saudi Arabia and jailed in Ukraine for murder.

TEN

Mushroom Story

I laughed remembering what Madhorupaagan had said on day one. 'An agent will go to great lengths to help the refugees cross the border, even if it means speaking the truth at times.' But this was no time to laugh. More recently, I had been learning some shocking truths. Or perhaps they were rumours. The number of abandoned elderly people in my area had been on the rise. They begged for survival. There were hundreds of street dogs that attacked pedestrians. There was a solution to both problems, I heard. To kill the street dogs and serve up their meat to the elders for free. The dog menace would end and the elders would survive.

I was terrified when I heard this.

Amma often wrote about drugs in her letters. She would end the letter warning me to be careful. I remembered the problem we had encountered at the apartment we had previously occupied. Abandoned elders and drug addicts would stay under the stairs without permission. Because it interrupted their sleep, they broke the lights with stones and would leave only when the security guard chased them away in the morning.

Thinking of all of this, I wondered what lay in store for me now. Madhorupaagan devised an elaborate plan to get me to Germany through Slovakia. There were plans to move a thirteen-member group. Normally, a plan with a large contingent always ended in failure. But Madhorupaagan said he had struck a deal with the guards at the border. However, that did not necessarily mean that the people he had struck a deal with would be on duty at the border on the day the contingent landed there, because the guards worked on a rotational basis. Left with no option, I joined the group.

Because I was now an expert in making student visas, many agents were my friends. One of them loaned me his travel permit document for five hundred dollars. It was a government document for refugees without a passport. I could travel anywhere with it except to my home country. I had to now change the photograph in the document to mine. There were experts to do this too. The understanding with the agent was to return the document soon after I landed in Germany.

The train arrived, and as soon as we boarded it, Eswaranathan bought dried mackerel as if he was waiting for it, and started eating it. The others did the same. The train smelt of dried fish. I thought of Pushpanathan. He would binge on dried mackerel. I recalled how Pushpanathan had thought of his twenty-three-year-old daughter as a child and asked me to post chocolates to her. As the train approached Mukachevo station, I grew nervous. I had once been caught there. Those who had caught and beat me up could still remember my face. If only I could cross this hurdle, I would be able to enter Czechia through Slovakia and reach Germany where an old friend was living. We were very close at one point of time. An agent had passed on my telephone number to him. 'Come, my friend.

Unwashed plates in Germany are waiting for you,' my friend wrote. He had not changed and had the same sense of humour.

When Mukachevo arrived, I left the group and stood alone. The railway guard gave my travel document a cursory glance without a word. I was surprised. The back of my head was still within reach. No one had touched it yet. He started inspecting the documents of the others. The remaining twelve members of the group were made to deboard the train. It never struck the officer that I could be one of them. When the train left, Eswaranathan screamed my name and waved at me. I didn't even look back.

There were agents waiting in Slovakia to take me to Germany. On reaching Germany, I called up my friend Sathyan. I was momentarily terrified at the thought of Sathyan not turning up. But he came, humming a song: you have come to the West / you have come to the West. 'You are a free bird now,' he said and hugged me.

Sathyan was full of stories. In his small room, Sathyan was lying on his bed and I on a mattress on the floor. The mattress had probably been used by a horse before me—it was hard and knotty. But I wasn't going to complain.

Sathyan suddenly got up and asked me, 'Do you know the story of the Russian president Khrushchev?'

When I replied in the negative, he started laughing without narrating the story.

'I can laugh along, if you share the story with me,' I said. But Sathyan was like that. Like Lavanya, he would laugh thinking of a joke before he shared it.

'One morning, Khrushchev wished the sun good morning. The sun wished him back. In the afternoon, he wished the sun good afternoon. The sun wished him back. In the evening, Khrushchev wished the sun good evening.

'"You silly idiot, I am in the west now," the sun said.

'Do not forget, you are in the West now,' Sathyan said, kicked me and laughed.

Sathyan used to wash plates at a restaurant for a living. He had filed for an appeal after his application for asylum was rejected. But there wasn't a jot of worry on his face. 'Friend, let us do happy things today. The rest can wait for tomorrow. Because no one knows what will happen in the future.'

He got me a job in the same restaurant. Sathyan had a Turkish girlfriend called Sameera. She too washed plates in the same restaurant. There was no dearth of food at the restaurant. Sathyan and I returned home at ten that night after he finished. There was a bus stand in front of the church. 'Remember the church,' he told me. Because every bus stand looked the same. The next morning, we had to leave for work at seven. I was happy but still had something to worry about. I did not have any documents. I had sent the travel permit back to its owner. If caught by the police, I would either be jailed or deported.

Sathyan's Turkish girlfriend would sometimes visit our room on Sundays. I had never seen something as black as her hair. The hair that lay in waves with no help from a hairdresser. Her head and neck were like a tulip on a long stem. Her eyes looked misty, even when she was smiling. Sameera would buy small lies but refused to believe the big truths.

'Ours is a poor village. At night, we would trap fireflies in a bottle and use them as light,' Sathyan would say, and she would believe him.

'Whales inject milk into the air and its calves drink it by catching it with their mouths.' She wouldn't believe that.

She would sometimes cook Turkish food. Mostly corba soup, made of lentils and tomatoes. She would worry about not having the most important ingredient.

'Goat's tongue,' she'd say when asked.

'That's fine, let the goat speak for a few more days,' Sathyan would say.

After the meal, we would go out for a stroll. The conversation between Sathyan and her was interesting: a mix of German, Turkish and English.

'How do you speak these languages?' I asked Sathyan once.

'Idiot, love doesn't need any language.'

'It's difficult to fathom the soul of a woman. They are deceptive. What is the secret of your love?'

'Simple! Stay by your girlfriend's side when she is crying. If you leave, your love will also leave.'

Sameera could be forgiven for her soup. But sometimes she would start making lunch. Mushrooms were the main ingredient in any meal she made. She could not cook without them. I would beg her not to cook mushrooms—in Ukraine, several refugees had died after consuming poisonous mushrooms—but she paid no heed. Sathyan asked if I knew the story of mushrooms and started laughing. 'Enough, tell me the story,' I said.

'One day a woman was at the cemetery, crying by a tombstone for a long while. "You could have eaten it, I told you, you could have eaten it," she kept saying. The cemetery guard asked her if he had died of starvation. "No, he was my fifth husband and he died so young."

'"How did he die?"

'"His head was smashed into four pieces."

'"How did your first husband die?"

'"He died from eating a poisonous mushroom."

'"Second husband?"

'"He too died of poisonous mushrooms."

'"The third one?"

'"Of course, from eating poisonous mushrooms."

'"And the fourth?"

'"How many times should I tell you? He also died of mushroom poisoning."

'"And the fifth one?"

'"Didn't I tell you already? He refused to have my mushroom soup, so I hit him just once with a hammer. His head broke into four pieces."'

I laughed along with Sathyan. Sameera did not laugh. She exacted her revenge by adding more mushrooms to the meal that day.

When Sameera had to send off her sister, Sathyan accompanied her and so did I. Sameera and her sister were walking ahead, speaking in Turkish. Sathyan did not like them talking in Turkish. He asked me in a loud voice, 'Do you know the story of a Turkish girlfriend?'

I said no.

It was now clear that the two women walking in front stopped their conversation and started listening to him intently.

'A Turkish woman was in love with a German. One day the German asked his girlfriend if the moon was full that day.'

'How would I know? I am from Turkey.'

Sathyan and I couldn't control our laughter. Sameera didn't laugh. 'I like you, but only fifty per cent,' Sameera's sister told Sathyan.

'This woman seems nice. She is a refugee and so are you. Where else will you find such a good match? Why don't you get married?' I asked Sathyan in a hushed tone.

'I too am thinking about it. If I was a writer, I would have married her by now.'

'Why is that?'

'A writer got divorced here in Germany. The woman asked for half his property. Ten thousand copies of his last novel remained unsold for ten years. He made an estimate of half of his property and gave away the books to her, claiming they were half his wealth. Today neither she nor the novels are around. The man is happy.'

Now it was my turn. I started chasing Sathyan and he ran away. The sisters were surprised at us two clowns.

One could spend any number of hours in a railway station. The trains would keep arriving at and leaving from different platforms. The passengers boarding the trains and getting off from them were fun to watch. So many kinds of human beings—white, black, brown, yellow—were seen there. So many languages were heard. So many types of clothes, accessories and gaits!

A young woman had left the first three buttons of her shirt open. Another had her multi-coloured stockings up to her thighs. Then I figured they weren't stockings; her legs had been tattooed all over with inks of different colours. As soon as Sameera's sister left, Sathyan, she and I had coffee. A train had just arrived and a woman boarded it. Many passengers were getting down. The woman waved to a handsome young man. I looked at her by accident. It was certainly Ahalya. She was dressed in modern attire and her hair was well-groomed. She had the same protruding eyes. Even after the train began to move, she was waving without realising it. I ran towards the train. I ran even after the train had disappeared. Suddenly, I felt ashamed of my folly and came to a dead stop.

Seeing that I was standing as if planted by someone in that spot, Sathyan shook me back to reality and took me away. He was aware of Ahalya's story. 'Why do you bother about someone who has left you already? She's no longer in your life. Forget her,' he said.

I knew those eyes. They were brimming with love. Once, standing under the Orion constellation, she had looked at me too in the same way.

That night, I could not sleep thinking of her. Did she ask her new lover about the sunrise every day? Did she think of me when she looked at the Roman numerals on her watch? Deciding that I should not be in the same city as her, I began searching for ways to leave.

ELEVEN

Refugee Magistrate

There was yet another Tamil working at Sathyan's restaurant. His name was Masilamani. People called him 'Masi'. Sathyan called him Annan (elder brother) and so did I. He was about thirty years old and strangely uncommunicative. I thought he carried a story deep within his heart, the weight of which flashed in his eyes, continuously; they constantly flickered, as if he were searching for something.

One day after restaurant hours, the three of us went out for a few beers. I was keen to know Masi's story, but Masi was silent. I was reminded of Jayakaran. Who could forget his long story or the immigration official derisively calling him the 'son of a chameleon'?

After the second beer, I asked Masi, 'Annan, how did you end up here? Everyone has a story. You always look sad. Won't you tell us? It'll make you feel better.'

'Mine is a long story,' began Masi, 'I feel weighed down by not just my story, but the story of my friend too. It's an unforgettable one. Okay, I'll tell you—but listen without interrupting.'

'I thought I would make a decision after reaching Bombay from Colombo. In 1985, I was nineteen. Czechoslovakia had not yet been partitioned. Russia's Aeroflot flew to East Berlin through Prague. Inexpensive visas to Prague were available in Bombay, so I bought one and took the flight. When I landed in Germany, it was February, and it was freezing cold.

'No book, no film can prepare a person from Asia for the European winter or its icy storms. Overcoats, boots and gloves will do nothing to fight the cold. I realised this immediately upon arriving at East Berlin's Schoenfeld Airport. The cold pierced my cheap overcoat and broke my bones. My fingertips were numb. The sounds I produced were not forming words. In the freezing air, my nose began to run. I had to remove my gloves to wipe it, but just couldn't do it. The water from my nose had turned to ice. When I spat, my spit falling on the ground made a thudding noise.

'I bought a twenty-four-hour visa for East Berlin for ten dollars, took a train to West Berlin and reached the Zoological Garden station, as per the instructions I had received. From there, I bought a ticket and boarded a train to Paris. But my destination wasn't Paris. The train would pass through Frankfurt and I would have to alight there. If the police caught me, I would be lodged at a refugee camp. From there, I reached a small town whose name sounded like "Eskirshon", where my friend Devan, three years junior to me, was living. If I managed to reach his place, he had promised to take care of my refugee status.

'I went with Devan and registered as a refugee. I could now live rent-free. Also, I would get a refugee stipend of 350 marks every month. We stayed in a two-room flat in an old building. Devan and I shared one room. A sixty-year-old man whom people called Master was in the other room. There was another thirty-three-year-old occupant whom people addressed as Magistrate. At first, I thought they were teasing him. But it turned out that he had been a real magistrate in Colombo, and had to flee soon after the war broke out. If a magistrate had to suffer such a fate, ordinary people like me didn't stand a chance?

'The four of us stayed in that flat for about a year and a half. Those were the happiest days of my life. We had no responsibilities and no jobs. We received our refugee allowance every month, sent half of it back home and spent the rest. However much we spent, there was still something left at the end of the month. So we put our savings together and bought a video deck. Tamil movies were just trickling into the market. Our first Tamil film in Germany was *Aan Paavam*, featuring Pandiyarajan. The film ran for twenty-five straight weeks; it was a silver jubilee. Since we played the same cassette again and again until we got the next one, it was a silver jubilee for us too.

'Beer was available in packs of six or twenty-four. We would watch the film, drinking beer. When high, Master would call out, "Hey, you Magistrate!" We often had small fights but forgot them almost immediately. No matter how intoxicated we were, we would still call him Magistrate anna. He was more educated than all of us put together and was highly intelligent. He knew all the laws. Once I saw him reading a book so huge that it was impossible to hold the front and back covers together with one hand.

'"What book is that?"

'"It's the story of how the Dutch ruled Ceylon, the old name for Sri Lanka. You should read it."

'"This heavy book?"

'"Isn't it about 138 years of Dutch rule?"

'"It will take me 138 years to complete it."

'Sometimes, when we were bored, we worked on the sly for wages. As refugees drawing money from the government, we weren't allowed to work. Devan went to pick strawberries at the farms in the villages nearby. They would pay him by weight. He would chat with Turkish women who, like himself, came to work as refugees. He wouldn't go to the farm the next day since his hands got sore. But conversations about the Turkish women continued in our flat.

'I washed plates in a restaurant—a tough, boring, laborious job. The owner wouldn't let the customers look at us. But we looked at them through a gap in the partition. We could see smooth, round legs under the tables. Some legs would be adorned in black, fishnet stockings. When rinsing plates, I would picture the women who would have eaten off them.

'Master was very hard working; in Jaffna, he used to take tuitions. His father made wedding stages and rented them out. In Germany, too, Master did not sit idle. He made two ceremonial wedding stages and rented them out. One of them was made of coloured beads and the other of artificial flowers. The refugees from Ceylon were now falling in love and getting married. Whenever Master got an order, Devan and I tagged along and helped him set up the stage. Those two days would be happy ones. We enjoyed it so much that every time we returned from a wedding, we would start dreaming of the next order for a wedding platform.

'Magistrate anna had a strange habit. Like an old-fashioned Jaffna lawyer, he had hung a nameplate with IN and OUT signs outside the door. When he was not at home, the OUT sign would be displayed. For two days every month, he would disappear, turning the OUT sign face up on the door. Nobody knew where he went or for what. Nor did we probe him. But when he returned, he would be in a state of bliss. He brought with him a bottle of high-end liquor and threw a lavish party. On that day, he would take over the kitchen. Having learnt the art of cooking somewhere, he produced an exquisite meal. But this was only once a month. On other days, it was Master who cooked. Devan and I helped him. When life in Germany became dull, we began to yearn for a change.

'It was true that the winter made us miserable. We spent our days next to the fireplace. But Germans were different. Their children played with snowballs. They made snowboards and slid on the snow. When spring came, an incident that impacted each one of us in different ways occurred.

'The trees were blooming again. The blood frozen in our bodies started circulating. An element that for ages aided the fertility of the human race made its entry silently. We felt a deep and inexplicable melancholy, a feeling of loss and despair.

'Then one night at ten p.m, we had just finished our dinner and were getting ready for bed when there was a knock on the door. I sat upright. At this hour? Who could it be? Visitors always announced their arrival over the phone in advance. Magistrate anna closed his heavy book. Devan leapt towards the door to open it. There was an excitement on his face at the thought of a new visitor. When he opened the door, I looked at Magistrate anna's starry eyes instead of the visitors at the door. It was a rare sight for refugees like us in Germany. The man was around fifty-five years of age, and bald. It was evident from his attire that he had spent at least a decade in Germany. The young woman with him gave us a real shock. She was around twenty-two and was wearing a sari. She had adorned her hair with flowers and her forehead was marked with kumkum, as if she was headed to a temple. She had long, luxuriant hair—so thick that no one could hold it all even with both hands.

'The four of us stood with mouths agape—reacting differently in accordance with our age, background and experience. No one spoke.

'Devan was the first to recover. His open mouth broke into a wide smile as he welcomed them. The woman's sister was getting married and they required a wedding stage. Lacking a proper address for our place, they had been searching for us for two hours.

'Master showed them sketches of his wedding stages. The woman was not impressed. She spoke to her father in German: "The wedding stage décor should be done with real flowers, not artificial ones." Before Master could open his mouth, Magistrate anna butted in, "We could do that, not a problem", as if he was the owner of this enterprise.

'Since the last train had already left, it was decided that the father and daughter would stay the night with us. Magistrate anna started cooking on his own. Our kitchen always had four things in stock: rice, lentils, chicken and yogurt. The meal was ready in half an hour and Magistrate anna laid the table. He did not allow us near the table, treating the food as if it was nuclear waste. Though Devan and I were ready to help, it was as if he had built a wall of security around himself, thinking that we would rob him of credit.

'The father and daughter were seated opposite each other at the dining table and Magistrate anna served them. She picked up the food with her slender fingers and slipped it into her mouth. We could see the ball of food going down her throat through her milky skin. At one point, she pouted as if she was ready to kiss.

'"Is it hot?" Magistrate anna asked her.

'"*Ja,*" she said. The first word she spoke to him.

'Devan beat me in a race to fetch her a glass of water. Magistrate anna took it away from him and handed it over to her, staring into her dark eyes. "*Danke,*" she said, but forgot to hold the glass.

'The laws of physics were the same across the colleges of Colombo where Magistrate anna had studied, Germany and anywhere else in the world. The glass hit the wooden floor and rolled across it. It did not break, though. "Nothing! It's just water—nothing!" Magistrate anna cried, going down on his knees to clean the floor, and looking intently at her feet.

'"*Es tut mir leid,*" said her lips, but her eyes were fixed on Magistrate anna. Not noticing any of this, her father served himself again. As he selected a chicken leg, he said, "Bhavani, have your meal dear."

'"Bhavani, Bhavani"—all of us uttered the name silently at the same time. Magistrate anna was thrilled to learn her name—it rolled off the tongue!

'The next morning, Magistrate anna, Devan and I went to the railway station to see them off. Dressed impeccably and exclusively for the send-off, Magistrate anna had nudged me at least four times to bring the camera. Even Devan was aware that there was a love story in the making, running faster than the train that would carry Bhavani and her father. Magistrate anna was keen to talk to Bhavani but wasn't sure what to say. The conversation did not move beyond monosyllables like *Ja* and *Danke*. When the train arrived, Bhavani and her father boarded it. Magistrate anna nudged me for the fifth time. When the train began to move, Bhavani looked at him and smiled. Then she turned and smiled at all of us. I clicked.'

'Germany's popular dog, the German Shepherd prepares for winter by shedding its hair and growing a new coat. It renews its look and appears handsome. Magistrate anna was just like that. He stopped reading and started talking. He ordered fresh flowers through a friend in Holland. Besides helping Master in getting the wedding stage ready, he also accompanied us to the wedding venue.

'Bhavani's sister wasn't particularly beautiful, but everyone at the wedding had a word of praise for the stage decorations. When returning home by train, Magistrate anna told me that he had received an answer.

'"What answer?"

'He said that he had given Bhavani akka a letter when she had visited us two months ago and had received her reply today.

'"And? Her answer?"'

It was time to close the bar. The workers were upending the chairs. Everyone was keen to know what had happened to the magistrate.

'I will share the rest of the story tomorrow,' Masi said and stopped.

TWELVE

28,000 Guilders

The following day, Masi Annan downed some beer and resumed his story without any reminders.

'Magistrate anna found it crucial to talk privately to me and wanted to leave Master out. Devan was a youngster. But Devan and I would discuss Bhavani akka without Magistrate anna's knowledge. Between us, we called her "*Danke* Bhavani". In front of Magistrate anna, we would politely refer to her as Bhavani akka.

'One day when we were alone, Magistrate anna told me, "I need nothing else in life but to hold Bhavani's dark tresses in my hands like I would hold flowing water." I thought it was time this man had a brain transplant.

'Bhavani akka became the subject of our everyday conversation at the dinner table.

'"Hey Magistrate, listen," said Master in some agitation one day. "What are you doing reading all those useless, big books? Of what use are you to anyone? Look at Devan. He picks fruits, braving the thorns. Look at Masi, he washes plates used by German women. You! You sleep all the time. Surely you've read that a running ant is better than a sleeping elephant. Get married to Bhavani soon. She is beautiful. I will gift you a memorable wedding stage made of natural flowers."

'Magistrate anna used to take me along whenever he stepped out. By his side, I looked even stupider than I usually did. He was unable to think about anything other than Bhavani. Over the two or three kilometres we walked, he would talk only about Bhavani. He said that he talked to her on the phone once a week. Once, on our walk, we bought two bacon sandwiches and coffee in paper cups. He began to munch on the sandwich. Suddenly two policemen twice our size landed in front of us and asked for our papers. My knees trembled at the sight of them. They left saying "Danke" after Magistrate anna showed them our papers.

'"Why are you afraid? When our civilisation was at its peak, Germans were still dancing wearing feathers on their heads."

'"But now they feed us every month by giving us refugee allowance," I said.

'"Those who silently witness a sin being committed anywhere in this world are also guilty of the sin."

'Standing on a carpet of leaves fallen the previous day, I pondered over Magistrate anna's words. The next day, against his name on the door was displayed an OUT sign. When he came back two days later, he was carrying a bottle of Chivas Regal. He cooked a huge meal on that day, but Master and Devan had gone out to buy some things. The food lay on the table, untouched. Magistrate anna drank more than he usually did and suddenly started to weep.

'"Magistrate anna, why are you crying?"

'"Brother, I remembered my mother. She died six months after I arrived here. All the letters I wrote to her were found under her pillow. I ran away to save myself, without thinking of her. I am a traitor, brother."

'"It's over, Magistrate anna. Think of the future."

'"My mother's biggest fear was that our family lineage would end with me. Fearing this she sent me abroad. She wanted me to get married and have a son. Only then would her soul rest in peace."

'"So what's the problem? Bhavani akka is ready and waiting for you."

'"You won't understand," he said, went to his room, and fetched a large card from his suitcase.

'"Look at this, this is our lineage. Long ago in my ancestral village, we had bards who would sing our family history. The story of our lineage was documented. When the war started, we moved houses many times and lost it. My mother wrote this from her memory."

'I looked at it. It appeared like a family tree. There were names and years beneath other names.

'"This is me, Thambirasa, born in 1950. This is my father Shanumuganathan, born in 1924. This is his father. The great grandfather of my great grandfather was Kanakarayan. He was born in 1784. His father's name was Mayilvaaganam. He was the origin of our lineage. He was the patriarch. I will name my child Mayilvaaganam, because that was where we began."

'"What is the problem then, Magistrate anna? You can name the child you have with Bhavani akka Mayilvaaganam."

'"Idiot, you don't know history, that's why you say such things. Mayilvaaganam was a hugely rich man. He was a pearl fishing contractor when we were ruled by the Dutch. In 1784, when Kanakarayan—the great grandfather of my great grandfather—was born, there was a huge famine. The Dutch rulers did nothing. Mayilvaaganam opened his paddy godown for the people, and they venerated him like a king. The news reached Wilken Faulk, the governor in Colombo. He arrested Mayilvaaganam and offered to release him only on payment of six thousand iraisaal. Mayilvaaganam had no option but to sell his house, property and farms. Our lineage never prospered after that."

'"It's an old story, Magistrate anna, let it go. Let's eat before the food gets cold."

'"You focus only on food," he said angrily. "You don't understand. The Dutch ruled us for 138 years and robbed my ancestors of their wealth. There is nobody to question this injustice."

'"We are refugees. This country pays us for being refugees. We have to build our future here. You know all the nuances of the law from those huge books. Forget the past, there is no way you can settle scores with the Dutch now."

'"Why not? I have been doing it! I have been doing it," he screamed. Then he fell asleep in his chair without eating.

'The next day, he remembered nothing. I reminded him. "Brother, my mother would always recollect a story about our ancestor Mayilvaaganam. She believed that I possessed his intellect. Once, when Mayilvaaganam was a seven-year-old child, a Dutch official and a local elder visited the family at the same time. Mayilvaaganam's father had gone out, so his mother gave two rolled betel leaves and asked the child to welcome both the men. The boy gave a rolled betel leaf to the Dutch official and the second one to the local elder with joined hands. Both the men were pleased."

'"Did you give the betel leaf to the Dutch official first because he is a White man? his mother asked."

"'I gave it to the Dutch man first so that I could greet the local elder with both my palms pressed together. I made both of them happy, he said."

"'That is what we call wit, brother. It should come naturally."

"'You spoke about avenging all that brutality done by the Dutch. What did you mean, Magistrate anna? I lost sleep last night thinking about it," I asked.

"'I will tell you. You are the first to hear this secret. Don't take the Dutch lightly. At one time, they ruled the world. They ruled parts of India and Ceylon. They captured South Africa and ruled it. They ruled the Philippines, and Suriname in South America. They established a giant empire, stretching from the West to the East. Just think about it. Holland is a small country, smaller than Ceylon. Twenty per cent of their land is below sea level. They travelled six thousand miles to enslave Ceylon. How many soldiers would the ship have carried? Two hundred or five hundred. With an army as small as that, they captured an entire country and ruled it. What tyrants they were! Willing to plunder other countries for the prosperity of their own.

"'Three years ago, I registered as a refugee in Germany. One day I took a train and reached Assen station, near the Dutch border. I took a taxi from there to reach Wasler Road. The border that divides Holland and Germany is 370 miles long. Once you get to Wasler Road, you can cross the border and reach Holland. There are no check points at the border. In Germany, the roads are lit by mercury lights and in Holland, the road lights are yellow. When I crossed the border, it was one a.m. The only danger could be the drug mafia. I shouldn't be caught by them. The Holland station is called Maastricht. From there, I bought a ticket to Amsterdam, went to the foreign police station and registered myself as a refugee. I identified myself as Mayilvaaganam Kanakarayan. The officers did not ask to see any documents. They immediately gave me a thousand guilders as refugee allowance. It is equivalent to thirty thousand rupees in Sri Lankan currency. Since that day, I visit them once a month and receive a thousand guilders as refugee allowance. I don't have a country of my own, but I am a refugee in two countries."

'I had no words to express my shock on hearing this. "Anna, you have studied the law. You have worked as a magistrate. Is it not wrong to cheat a country out of money? It's not just illegal but inhuman too," I told him.

'"What is illegal about this? I'm getting what they owe me. I'm reclaiming the money that my ancestors lost to them. I'm not going to do this forever. I have already sent 26,000 guilders to the orphanage in my mother's name in Jaffna. Another two months and it will be 28,000 guilders, and the Dutch will have repaid all the money due to me. And then I will stop."

'I never shared this secret with anyone. It was decided that Magistrate anna's wedding with Bhavani akka would take place after six months when she finished her course in pharmacology. For the first time, Magistrate anna informed me before leaving for Holland. "Today is Sunday. Tomorrow is Monday. I will be back on Tuesday by sunrise."

'"Anna, be careful. There is a soul waiting here for you now. Recently, there was a debate in the Dutch Parliament about two people swindling money by duping the immigration authorities. What you've recovered so far is enough. Why should you go now?"

'"No, my friend. I will be careful. This mission has to be accomplished. I will stop at 28,000 guilders," he said.

'This time, he forgot to change the IN sign to OUT before he left. On that day, Devan, Master and I left for the supermarket. I think it was autumn, maybe the September of 1986. The weather was pleasant. It was still bright after the sunset, but the German moon was out. German leaves were flying in the German air. I thought it was very romantic. My heart soared in happiness. We had got the refugee allowance and bought our groceries for the month. Magistrate anna had not returned to house number 55, Hilton Street yet. He should have been back on Tuesday morning. The IN sign hung on the door for a long time.

'When my refugee application was rejected, I looked for another place, joined another set of friends and started a new chapter. Life in Euskirchen city came to an abrupt end. I felt I had got down from the train too soon, before my station had arrived. I stood now where I had started, not knowing where life would take me next. But despite that uncertainty and sadness, I couldn't help but think of Magistrate anna and what became of him.'

Masi opened his wallet and showed me a photograph that he had saved for several years. Of a woman waving from a train. Her beauty shone even through that faded photograph. Her father looked at the camera unsmilingly. The back of Magistrate alias Thambirasa's head and raised hands could be seen too. His face, which sought to reclaim the debts that the Dutch owed his ancestors eight generations ago, wasn't visible though.

THIRTEEN

Belgian Sun

Masi Annan's story filled me with an inexplicable dread. I became obsessed with a single thought: to somehow leave. Two employees—one Sudani and the other Kurdish—had decided to go to Belgium through an agent, and from there to England. How many more, chased away from their roots like them, were still searching for a country? I decided to go with them.

'Please don't go,' Sathyan pleaded with me. 'Sameera will stop cooking mushrooms, I promise you that. I assure you, I give my word. I guarantee you, it is a commitment,' he stopped, for want of new words. I had six hundred marks in my pocket—money saved from washing plates.

'Hundreds of them cross the borders without any problem,' the agent said. What he left unsaid was that two hundred odd people were caught every day, trying to cross the border.

The agent took us at two in the morning. He stopped after reaching the border, parked the car and waited for a signal. Policemen surrounded a huge, heavy vehicle on its arrival and held a lengthy investigation. When the agent started the car again, the police officer gestured to him to go ahead. We crossed the border. How easy was that? How many times had I tried to cross the Ukraine – Slovakia border and failed? And now, without any hurdle, I had crossed the German border and stepped into Belgium. With sufficient money and the right contacts, one could travel across the border between any two countries in the world.

We stayed in a small house owned by the agent in the suburbs of the city. There was no human activity in the area. At the mouth of the street, there was a postbox. Written on it was the long name of the road, starting with G and ending with L. The agent hardly spoke to us, yet everything happened as planned. As we stepped into his house, for a moment, I was stunned. There were people lying on the floor everywhere. There was a person lying even in the kitchen. These people were all on their way to different countries. There were large quantities of bread, butter and cheese on the table. Anyone could help themselves to the food. Tea was available in plenty. Nobody exercised any authority there, yet there was some kind of discipline. The silence was terrifying. No one spoke to anyone nor looked at another in the face. Strangely, everyone was immersed in their own worries. They looked like criminals in a movie, who appeared tense and pensive before a bank robbery.

On the 13th of January, the agent had asked us to be ready early. We could each take a small bag with us. The team of three started at around five o' clock. By the time it was beginning to get dark, we had entered the port. I later found out the name of the port: Seabrook. We did not know why we had been brought there by the agent. Waiting for the right opportunity, he drove the car in circles, and then suddenly, as the sky darkened, he swerved and stopped the car in front of a forty-five-feet-long container. We were all wearing jackets heavy enough to protect us from the biting cold. The agent gave us bottles of water, three packets of cakes and three balloons.

'You will know why later,' the agent said, when we asked him about the balloons. He gave me a knife and a torch. Removing the plastic curtain of the container, the agent sent us inside and said, 'Make no sound, and you will reach Britain's Tower port on this ship this very day. As soon as you reach, make a request for refugee status. Don't ever mention my name.'

He replaced the plastic curtain. It was dark inside the container. Only then did I remember that the agent had never once mentioned his name.

I had trouble communicating with the others who had come with me. One, it was too dark to see each other and two, language; the three of us had no language in common. Three, even if they spoke in hushed tones, the echoes inside the shut container were strong. Nothing happened until midnight. We fell asleep, then woke up. The agent had said that the container would be loaded on a vessel at night. We could hear the sound of other containers being loaded and also watch them through a small tear in the plastic curtain. Our container stood still. We could hear footsteps and a dog barking outside. The guard probably had doubts. The dog's barks grew louder as it drew closer. The guard chided the dog and pulled it away, but he came back and inspected the container. We were hiding behind tall piles of boxes, so he didn't see us and left.

It was morning now. The sounds of the morning were different. We were hungry. We had the cakes and drank water. Heavy vehicles passed by. We could hear the sounds of people up close. I climbed upon the boxes, flashed my torch and looked around. I counted 150 boxes of huge underground cables. The delivery address said they were going to Poland from England. The container wasn't bound for England. It had come from England. The agent had loaded us into the wrong container by mistake.

The others too soon realised what had happened. We were wondering what to do when the vehicle started moving. We were travelling towards Poland. The vehicle picked up speed as soon as it reached the main road. I cut the curtain open and thrust my face out. The Belgium sun was starting a new day.

The sunlight washed my face. I remembered that it was the day of Pongal. Amma would celebrate the day by offering milk and rice to Sun God. My sister would be looking at the same sun as I. Perhaps, Ahalya too.

I jumped off the vehicle when it stopped at the next traffic signal, and so did the others. Holding our bags, we ran in the opposite direction. The signals turned green in time, and the truck left for Poland with 150 boxes of underground cables and three balloons filled with urine.

It was then that we looked at each other's faces. We went to a coffee shop and had coffee. Putting all our money on the table, we counted it. We called the agent from a public telephone booth, but the call went unanswered. We were now very hungry and couldn't remember the agent's address. We had no option but to walk.

An old woman was cleaning the coffee shop. She kept looking at us curiously, even while mopping the floor. We wondered whether she would hand us over to the police. We decided to leave and rushed out. But we didn't know which direction to take; we also didn't know the language so as to make enquiries. The old woman followed us out and handed over a bag with bread, fruit and water. We could not believe our eyes. She appeared to be the incarnation of all the mothers in the world. I was crying. The three of us stood in front of her, palms pressed together. We didn't know how else to thank her.

After walking for several hours, at around ten p.m., we found a street that had a postbox. The name of the street started with G and ended at L. Upon seeing us, the agent smacked his head. A problem he couldn't have imagined even in his wildest dreams had cropped up. The agent realised his mistake. The Sudani and the Kurd were ready to depart the next day in another container heading for England. I refused to go with them. I requested the agent to send me back to Germany instead. The only good thing that came of this long journey: I was able to see the shining Belgium sun on the most auspicious day of Pongal.

I crossed the Belgian border in a car arranged and paid for by the agent and entered Germany. I took a bus, got down at the bus stop opposite the church, and started walking towards Sathyan's flat.

FOURTEEN

Stone House

'Eat after counting your money.' I remembered the advice my grandfather had given me a long time ago. 'If you eat before you count your money, you will end up doing a menial job at a restaurant or in some jail.' I should have thought about that a bit more before leaving Germany. It was no use thinking about it now.

I arrived in Paris to carry out an important assignment for the agent. He had a language problem in both places. It was up to him to think about what to do next. Nobody else could do the thinking for him.

Finding me reliable, the agent had summoned me to entrust me with an important assignment: I was to travel to Rome to fetch someone. I laughed at the suggestion. I was uncertain about what to do next, but the agent was serious about sending me to Rome.

'Why can't *you* do that?' I asked the agent.

'If there's a problem in *your* journey, *I* can set it right. What if I go to Rome and land in a fix? Who will save me?' the agent retorted.

The person whom I was supposed to bring back was called Kanakalingam. 'If he could travel alone from Colombo to Rome, could he not travel to Paris from Rome? All he had to do was catch a train.'

'Nishant, don't ask so many questions. His son is in Canada and has paid a huge sum to bring him here. This man has a peculiar problem. If the immigration authorities ask him one question, he will give ten answers. He cannot stop himself from landing in trouble. His son is worried that his father will be sent back if he gets into trouble with his foolish responses. Kanakalingam already has a fake Canadian passport. I will give you one too. It is your responsibility to escort him safely to Paris. If you do this job for me, I will send you to Canada for free.'

I took a train to Rome. I didn't face any hurdles journeying in Europe. When I reached Kanakalingam's address, I found the house locked. I rang the bell several times, but nothing happened. I was tired and getting irritable, wondering what to do next.

At some distance, a person stood watching me. He slowly moved towards me and asked in chaste Tamil, 'What do you want?'

'I am looking for Kanakalingam.'

'That's me,' he said, with a laugh that sounded like a dog yelping when someone steps on its tail. He said he was hiding from someone he had borrowed money from and was temporarily staying with some friends.

'Welcome, welcome,' he said suddenly and started walking as if he was being chased.

Kanakalingam was about sixty, with dry, papery skin. Left untrimmed for a long time, his overgrown hair had reached his shoulders. He was tall, lanky and restless. His unwashed overcoat was smelly. The soles of his outsized shoes were torn and flapped when he walked. The shoes were not helping him. Rather, he was using his feet to carry them. I looked at his socks that were threadbare and offered no protection at all. They were probably older than him. I wondered how the agent would send *this* man to Canada.

With high-rise buildings on either side of the street we were walking on, there was no room for sunlight, and our shadows fell over each other. Kanakalingam lived with two people from Africa on the fourth floor of a building. His belongings were packed in a bag that had many holes. Anybody could be forgiven for viewing both him and his bag with suspicion.

Kanakalingam and I left for the station to buy tickets for Paris, but the soonest they were available for was three days later.

'Fine, give me the money,' I said. Kanakalingam looked all around, nervously, bent over and pulled the money out of his torn socks. We came back to the room after buying the tickets. The Africans were very kind and said we could stay with them rent-free for two days.

Left to himself, Kanakalingam appeared despondent, gazing at the floor, neck slumped like an eagle's. I felt sorry for him. I hardly knew what to do for the next two days. I could have asked him to take me sightseeing, but he was afraid of those to whom he owed money.

'You go—' he said. So I wandered throughout Rome, visiting the Vatican, the Colosseum and St. Peter's tomb, and when I returned, Kanakalingam and I went out for dinner.

'Do I look like an intellectual to you?' asked Kanakalingam.

I could see only a four-day-old beard on him, no intellectuality.

'Get me a beer,' he said. After buying him one, I realised it was a grave mistake. I remembered the agent mentioning how Kanakalingam was unstoppable once he got talking. Words streamed out of him like ribbons from the mouth of a magician.

'You know what I was doing in Colombo? I was a land surveyor. A land surveyor is very important for a country. Nobody knows this. Think about it. If the land is not surveyed, how can it be ruled? I surveyed the plots of more than half of the buildings in Colombo. Every building carries my name. Do you know that the land survey department has existed for two hundred years in Colombo? It was the first department to be established by the British. This department doesn't have a minister. Many people worked under me … and look at me today—roaming around in torn shoes.'

'Why do you have to go to Canada at this age? It is a cold country. Couldn't you have lived with your sister in Colombo?'

'I can share this with you, my friend. I have surveyed lands for many buildings. I cannot bear to see the fate endured by my sister and her four daughters. The military shot her husband dead. Every house on her street has a number, except my sister's. Do you know why? You need a door to have a number. She lives in a hut. If it rains, the water sweeps into half the house. Every year, the usable part of the house shrinks. When we sleep, worms creep out from beneath the floor. Jaffna has a species of bird called the fly catcher. It catches house flies and eats them throughout the day. Its stomach is always half empty. Our stomachs are the same. The only thing abundantly available in that hut is hunger. When my sister eats, her daughters keep staring at her, waiting to eat whatever she leaves on her plate. And whenever the daughters eat, my sister stares at them to eat their leftovers. How long could I turn a blind eye to their plight? I couldn't bear to see their suffering and decided to leave.'

'What are you going to do in Canada?'

'What kind of question is this? I'm going to build a stone house for my sister. I have to work for that. I will wash plates, deliver newspapers and sweep roads. I will do anything.'

'You cannot sweep roads there. There are huge machines to do that job.'

'So be it, I will then play the nadaswaram.'

'Nadaswaram, the musical instrument?'

'My friend, there are forty-seven temples in Canada. Even if I play the nadaswaram in four temples, I will earn enough to build my sister a house. I am ready to work.'

'Do you know how to play the nadaswaram?'

'I can learn. It's not magic, is it? It's all about blowing some air into the instrument.'

He drained his glass of beer and looked at me.

'What is this white liquid?'

'Gin, another kind of liquor.'

'Will it make me drunk?'

'This is enough for today,' I decided and we left.

Kanakalingam walked like a piece of paper flying in the air and I followed him.

The Africans gave us their beds and slept on the floor. They were Christians who had immigrated to Rome from South Sudan. They had applied for a stay visa and were waiting for it. Both of them were tall and so thin that their bones stuck out. Their breakfast consisted of bread and bananas. For lunch, they had tea; for dinner, soup and bread. They roamed around every day, looking at the city. They knew everything about the tourist spots. They would act as guides for African and Arab tourists and earn some money. Since they did not have permits, they were working on the sly for half the money guides usually charged. If their visa was granted, they planned to do it full-time.

'How did you come to choose this profession?' I asked.

'We have studied history the proper way. Here, they teach everything wrong,' they said.

I told them about my visit to St. Peter's tomb. At this, both of them turned emotional and wept uncontrollably. I felt bad about informing them of my visit.

'We visit the tomb once a month to offer our prayers. Jesus was interrogated. He was charged with declaring himself as the King of Jews. But what sin did St. Peter commit? There was no trial. His crime was being an apostle of Jesus. Before he was crucified, he had just one prayer. Jesus was crucified upright. Peter prayed to be crucified upside down, for he felt unworthy of dying in the same manner as Jesus. So he was crucified upside down.' Both the men wept again. Suddenly one started praying and the other repeated after him. Then, both of them fell asleep.

I couldn't sleep for a long time. How would Kanakalingam reach Canada? He was at once a child and an intellectual. His brain worked like a malfunctioning radio, intermittently coming to life. He said he would work in Canada and build a stone house. Why didn't he say he would survey lands and survive? He said he would play the nadaswaram. If he blew through one end, he said his breath would come out as music at the other end. Land measured the same anywhere in the world. If a land was a hundred feet in Colombo, wouldn't it be the same in Canada too? Wasn't surveying land a good job? Another thought frightened me. Kanakalingam would reach Canada before me. What did it matter if he surveyed land or blew air through the nadaswaram. He was certainly cleverer than me.

I thought about myself. Everybody was going ahead of me. Where would I be ten years from today? Jaffna? Paris? Canada? Or jail? The thought sent a shiver down my spine.

The next day, we travelled by train for ten hours. I felt like I was travelling with an eight-year-old child. Kanakalingam couldn't stop buying everything he saw. He bought soup, salad, chicken, etc. at various railway stations and ate them with relish. He bought ice-cream twice and licked them like a child. When he asked for beer, I refused. What if he blurted out something? Finally, I asked him, 'Instead of playing the nadaswaram in Canada, why not do land survey?'

'That's a good question, my friend. In Canada, I'll have to pass an exam to do land surveys. But to play the nadaswaram, I won't have to pass any exam. It is greatly respected in Canada, I am told. When you play the nadaswaram in a temple, no one will dare point out a mistake.

'In our town, there is scant regard for land surveyors. People view them as thieves. Like a tailor who uses physical measurements to stitch a beautiful garment from a piece of cloth, I use land measurements to draw up a plan. Land survey marked the start of civilisation. The practice began thousands of years ago in Egypt. A thousand years ago, a king known by the name of William the Conqueror surveyed and measured the whole of England and documented it. What a stupendous work that was! Written in black and red dyes on processed goat skin, and known as the Domesday Book, it still exists somewhere in a Cambridge museum. I should somehow see it before I die.'

'How many ambitions do you have? You want to visit the museum, you want to learn to play the nadaswaram, and then you want to build a stone house for your sister. Don't you think you are going a little overboard?'

'Are you mocking me, my friend? What's wrong with making plans and feeling happy about it? It is free after all. You don't know my story. I have carried a theodolite, a tripod stand and measuring tapes across long distances in Sri Lanka. I have worked in the sun, rain and wind. I have been chased away from Sinhala villages and then fed by them later on. I have even travelled with a crow.'

'A crow?'

'As soon as I picked up the theodolite, a crow would come and knock on the equipment with its beak just when I was about to finish the measurement. I would do all the measurements again and the crow would do the same once more. The crow stalked me for a week.'

'It must have been the soul of a person who opposed land measurements in their previous birth.'

'What do you think? Will I reach Canada? My son keeps tutoring me over the phone. Tells me not to say this or that. Nobody tells me what I *should* say.'

'All you have to do is to respond precisely to their questions. Say nothing more. Remember just that. Your son makes the same point.'

In ten hours, we reached Paris and I handed Kanakalingam over to the agent. We faced no problem during the journey. A new suitcase, shoes and an overcoat were bought for Kanakalingam. His hair, untrimmed for three months, was neatly styled. The young hairdresser wrinkled her nose while cutting his hair that was last cut in Colombo three months ago. The agent paid her an extra five francs. Kanakalingam's son kept calling the agent over the phone. Finally, one day, a decision on how to send Kanakalingam was made. He would fly from Charles de Gaulle Airport to Amsterdam, and from there, another flight would take him to Toronto. There would be no problem in flying to Amsterdam. But a huge hurdle awaited him at immigration in Amsterdam. They would allow him to board a flight to Toronto only after a thorough interrogation. If they discovered that his passport wasn't genuine, he would be sent back or imprisoned. If asked about his stay in Canada, he had to reply properly and with confidence. Why had he come to Paris? He should respond in a single sentence. If he answered in detail, they might have doubts. The agent trained him day and night.

On the day of his departure, the agent and I took him to Charles de Gaulle Airport. Kanakalingam was nervous. His ticket was checked and he was issued a boarding pass. He had to board now. Kanakalingam took me to a side and asked, 'What if they catch me and send me to prison in Amsterdam? What will I do then? How many years will it take for me to be released?'

'You shouldn't worry about these things. You are a Canadian citizen. Your passport says so. You shouldn't think like a Sri Lankan, you should think like a Canadian. You shouldn't be nervous when talking to them. Be confident.'

'All right, my friend. What is that colourless drink? Looks like water ...?'

'Vodka, a Russian drink.'

He struggled to make a decision, like a bee in front of a hundred flowers.

'It looks like water, it will not affect me. Get me a peg.'

I didn't tell him that the drink would leave him highly intoxicated, even if it looked like water. I felt sorry for him. Perhaps it would be his last glass of vodka in twenty years. I glanced at the agent. He was not to know! He would be livid if he did. I bought the vodka for Kanakalingam. Like a trained nadaswaram player raising his head and pointing the nadaswaram to the sky on a high note, Kanakalingam tossed his head back, opened his mouth and downed the vodka.

A few moments later, he said, 'This is good, my friend, get me another one. I will name the stone house I intend to build after you.'

In Sri Lanka, it was a practice to name houses after sons and grandsons. Kanakalingam said he would name his house after me. I thought there was no harm and bought him another vodka. Between each gulp, Kanakalingam smiled.

Then, leaving his bag behind, he walked away unsteadily. I ran after him and handed over the bag to him. He received it like he would from a servant, held the boarding pass above his head, waving it like a victory flag, and walked into immigration. I looked on, as if gazing upon him one last time.

That night, neither I nor the agent slept. We were waiting for the telephone call from Amsterdam that could come any moment now. The phone call never came. Kanakalingam was probably in jail. Even as we were wondering how to convey this to his son, we received a call from him. 'Thank you,' he said the moment the agent picked up the phone. 'Appa landed without any problem. He is still jet-lagged and sleeping.'

The agent was surprised. I was even more surprised. How had he managed to navigate the Amsterdam airport? What gimmicks did he pull off in Toronto? It was all a mystery.

Kanakalingam was drunk when he boarded the flight. On the flight, he had drunk more vodka because it was free. After that, he couldn't recollect landing in Amsterdam and answering questions at the immigration. He was allowed to fly to Toronto after his ticket and passport were examined. No questions asked. Even if they asked, Kanakalingam was in no position to answer. Even on reaching Canada, he was drunk. He was allowed into Toronto after he showed his passport at the immigration counter. His son met him and took him home. Usually someone travelling on a fake passport would be nervous. But Kanakalingam was not in the least nervous. Instead, those who somehow sent him to Canada and those who received him in Toronto were nervous.

After this incident, there was a change in the agent's attitude. Whenever he went to the airport to send off his customers, he told them to drink some vodka.

FIFTEEN

The Haunted Face

The agent was delighted, and he thought I was half the reason for a success he had not anticipated. Next he said, was to plan my own travel to Canada. Do we need a new plan, I wondered. The Amsterdam route appeared fine and I already had a passport that looked perfectly valid. But it was due to expire in a few weeks, so I had to reach Canada before that. Extending the expiry date was a complicated process. So once again, I was frustrated, and my worst fears came true. Travelling to Canada through Amsterdam became risky, because the agent's strategy had made an immigration official suspicious.

He noticed entirely by chance that many refugees were choosing this particular route. Their passport photographs did not always match their faces. Many were sent back and some were lodged in jails. That sealed off this particular route. When I pressurised him, the agent said he needed time to find another route. 'If your path is filled with salt, don't waste your time clearing it. Give it time and it will dissolve on its own.'

I got tired of waiting, though I knew the agent had to be cautious. Everybody had had an easy journey. Only when it was my turn, things became difficult. What happened in

Ukraine and Germany was repeating itself. Kanakalingam had reached without any problem. He would have probably learnt to play the nadaswaram by now and started performing in a few temples too. I wouldn't be surprised if Kanakalingam had already laid the foundation for his stone house, I thought bitterly, finding myself at the same point where I had started. The agent tried to comfort me by saying that in a hospital there were coloured lines on the floor: blue leading to the X-ray unit, yellow to cardiology and red to intensive care, etc. Such route maps could not be installed in our lives because things kept changing. It was like crossing a desert. Once you reached the other end, the path you had travelled on disappeared.

One day the agent came looking for me excitedly. I couldn't believe what the agent said. Apparently, there was a thirty-year-old woman with a fake Canadian passport, according to which her name was Sakunthala. She had tried to go to Canada three times but was caught halfway on every attempt and sent back. A huge amount of money had been spent on her already, so no agent was willing to touch her, the risk being far too great. If I agreed to accompany her, the woman's family was willing to sponsor my ticket to Canada. Her husband was in India. Her brother-in-law had taken her sons to Canada, registering them as his sons. Though determined to join her children, having failed multiple times to cross over had given her face a permanently nervous expression.

'It is your responsibility to take Sakunthala to Canada. Are you willing?'

I laughed at the agent, feeling helpless. I wondered how I could be made responsible for another human being in this perilous task but agreed.

The agent and I met the woman on a fixed date. I recognised her the moment I saw her. I had always visualised a face that was haunted, ashen. Here it was. Her face was pale with fear, as if she had been forced to sit close to a snake. When faced with a question, she took a long time to respond, as if the question had to travel a mile to reach her brain and elicit a response.

'This is my first visit to Canada. You should pose as my girlfriend; would you be all right with that?' I asked. She thought about it, head bowed. She thought about it, raising her head. She had no choice and wanted to somehow join her children. She looked down at the floor and dipped her head, meaning yes.

I pondered over the meeting on my return. In the one-hour meeting, not once had Sakunthala smiled. The immigration official would suspect her from ten feet away. Would a woman posing as a happy girlfriend look like she was walking towards the gallows? She should smile a bit.

'Doesn't she ever smile? Was she born this way? Or did something happen midway?' I asked the agent.

'Why do you worry about that? She is being her natural self. She won't smile even if an income tax official returns a million dollars saying she overpaid them. Don't train her to smile. Other bits of training are fine,' the agent said. She should learn to dress and speak like a Canadian. She had to memorise the names, addresses and dates of her journey as mentioned in the passport.

'When there are so many hurdles, how can I take a woman with me? They are going to send me back too,' I said, heartbroken.

The agent wasn't someone easily shaken. 'Nishant, yes, there *are* problems. But look at it this way—just because there is a risk involved in crossing a road, should we stop travelling? Success lies in sensing what lies ahead and handling it the right way.'

During our next meeting, I trained Sakunthala. I collected details about Canada and tutored her. We worked as if we were preparing for a major exam: Where to buy clothes in Toronto? What is the name of the bus stop near where we will stay? The names of three banks; the names of two hospitals. Who is your doctor? Do you have a credit card? How many nickels are there in a dollar? Sakunthala exerted herself and learnt everything. But the answers sometimes stuck in her throat when she was questioned. Her lips quivered. I felt pity for her.

A new path had opened up and was running successfully. The agent decided to send us off before any problems could arise. First, from Paris we would travel to Madrid in Spain. From Madrid to the Dominican Republic, and from there to Toronto. At the immigration in Madrid, we had to pose as a couple. First hurdle: How could I teach a woman who couldn't smile to act as if she was in love?

The agent gave me one last piece of advice before we stepped into Orly Airport. 'Don't let anyone know when you will reach Canada and by which flight.' I asked why. 'It is best to be cautious. Some people like to throw stones at a streetlight which does no one any harm. We cannot be sure that everyone will appreciate something good happening to someone else. You don't have to be an enemy for such people to spoil your plans.'

I responded to all the questions smoothly at the immigration counter. I said we were returning to Santo Domingo after a holiday in Madrid and showed our return tickets. When I said that, Sakunthala was supposed to drape her arms around my shoulders. She was not to utter a word. Sakunthala acted accordingly. There was only an inch of space between us. The immigration official checked our faces and the photos in the passports, and stamped our passports.

One hurdle crossed, two left.

We encountered no difficulty at the Santo Domingo airport. The place was full of tourists, so we were asked only two questions: how long will you be staying and where? I had ready answers for both. Taking a cab, we reached the hotel arranged by the agent in about ten minutes. It didn't look like a foreign country. There were many trees commonly found in Sri Lanka, like mango, papaya and jackfruit. The flowers too reminded us of Sri Lanka, like hibiscus and bougainvillea. The air carried the scent of salt. We felt a sense of freedom—as if we were being released from a prison.

I was happy. Canada was within my reach. This woman should cooperate. A small mistake could change our lives. I made it clear to the agent that we would pose as lovers only outside of Canada. Once the flight landed in Toronto, we would be strangers to each other. That was the safest thing for both of us. Sakunthala agreed wholeheartedly. We would stay in Santo Domingo for about a week, receive flight tickets for trips from Toronto to Santo Domingo and back by courier. We were lovers who had come to Santo Domingo for a vacation from Canada and were returning. This was the story. Only then would nobody doubt us when we landed in Toronto.

For the first couple of days, we ate out. Then Sakunthala got tired of it. If I forced her to come out, she would carry her sorrow like a flag on her head, and walk with her head drooping. Sometimes, she wept thinking of something. I would comfort her. I would tell her that it was only a matter of a few days. She would soon be in Canada and her problems would be at an end. She would nod in agreement. She wrote down all the points about Canada that she had been taught by the agent and me on a sheet of paper and started memorising them. I repeatedly told her that I could not help her at the immigration check post in Canada. Both of us knew that that was the safest thing for us.

One day, Sakunthala woke up before dawn to memorise facts about Canada. Suddenly she slapped her face with her hands and cried, 'I cannot do this, I cannot do this!' Tears ran through her fingers as she tried to wipe them off her face.

I panicked.

'My home address. Can't it be changed?'

'Why, what's the issue?'

'The name of my city here is Mississauga. I can neither read nor pronounce it.'

'How can we change the address? It is written in your passport. Stop worrying about it. Think about this: you will meet your children soon. These are minor issues. Come on, say this: Miss—iss—auga.'

In an hour, I taught her to pronounce the city's name.

The next day, Sakunthala spoke to her children over the phone. Her face changed completely when she was on the phone. 'I will arrive in the next two days. Don't forget me.'

The love on her face amazed me. Nobody who had looked at her face could imagine that it could glow with such love. I felt sorry for her and prayed that she would go past the immigration counter in Canada and be reunited with her children.

Every day, buying meals for Sakunthala was a problem. She was a vegetarian, so I could only buy her bread, bananas, vegetable soup, yoghurt or steamed rice. How long could she survive on them? She was tired of the food. Feeling bad for her,

I once bought noodles at a Chinese restaurant. The noodles had prawns in it. I ate all the prawns and gave the noodles to her. Sakunthala took an instant liking to the food. She asked for the same noodles the next day. On the third day, I had accidentally left a single prawn in the noodle dish. Sakunthala picked it up and held it close to her eyes. 'Fried mushroom,' I said. But she realised what it was after eating it. She wailed and wept and could not stop vomiting.

By midnight, she had fainted.

I ran to the reception but saw no one there. I ran back to the room and found Sakunthala still unconscious. I asked the security guard outside the hotel to call a taxi. 'We need to go to a hospital,' I said. The security guy understood only half of what I said. But he somehow managed to tell me that a doctor was staying in room number 8. I banged the door of room number 8 for a long time.

Was Sakunthala going to die? All her details would be public then. The media would write about it. I would be sentenced to death for the murder. I trembled. All kinds of thoughts ran through my mind. The door to room number 8 opened suddenly and a short, angry man in pyjamas stood before me. Luckily, the doctor knew a little English. Sakunthala lay unconscious in a pool of her own vomit. The doctor examined her and administered an injection. Then, we let her rest.

'Nothing to worry about, she will be all right,' the doctor said and left.

Sakunthala woke up at three in the afternoon. I gave her tea and biscuits. Suddenly, she got up and took a shower, changed her clothes and left the room. When I offered to accompany her, she refused. For two hours, she did not come back. I started cursing the agent for hooking me up with this strange woman. It grew dark. As I got ready to go and search for her, she returned to the room carrying a parcel. She opened the parcel and started eating her meal. The scent of sweet rice filled the room. She ate without looking at me, facing the wall.

How had she managed to find this meal? Had she been here before? Or did she know someone in Santo Domingo? Did she want to teach me a lesson? *'Didn't you try to kill me with noodles? There is sweet rice available here, don't you know even this?'* How worried I had been when she vomited. But she wasn't talking to me now. Would I ever have eaten alone if I had got my hands on sweet rice? I would have parcelled it for her. What kind of a woman was she?

When I was thinking along these lines, she washed her hands, took out another parcel from her bag, handed it over to me, and laughed loudly at my shocked expression. This was the first time she had laughed. It could be the last time too. Like leaves falling off a tree, her lips had smiled with no soul behind them. But her old face vanished and a new one now appeared. It looked nice too. That day turned out to be a happy one for both of us.

She had noticed a Hare Krishna procession in the city when we had travelled by cab from the airport. She visited the temple where they had distributed sweet rice after worship. How could a temple offering change her so much?

She volunteered her story. Her father was a farmer and was very attached to his two daughters. He got her married to a businessman who visited India often on work. When the Sri Lankan army was tightening its hold on Jaffna, her husband stopped coming back to the country. She had two children and had to struggle to raise them. When her husband's brother left for Canada, he took the children away with him, registering them as his children. She had tried to reach Canada several times but had been caught and sent back. This time she had to somehow reach her sons. This was her only prayer.

'What about your sister?' I asked.

'You may have read in ancient literature about young women eloping at night with their lovers. When they eloped, the sound of their anklets would give them away. So they would remove the anklets, hang them at the door and then run. The mother, on spotting the anklets in the morning, would start wailing. The same thing happened in my home. My mother discovered a pair of anklets hanging from the door one day. My sister had run away to join the freedom struggle. In 1987, she figured in the list of women fighters who had died following Malathy's martyrdom.'

We received our tickets by courier from Toronto for a flight scheduled for the next day. We arrived at the airport by three p.m. for the seven p.m. flight. We roamed around the airport like young lovers. Sakunthala had changed completely. There was a spring in her step and she was smiling a lot.

'I don't know if Canada will take me in or not, but I will never forget you,' she said.

'Nothing to worry about, just be careful about pronouncing Mississauga,' I responded.

We approached a youth walking along and enquired about the ticket counter. Without breaking the stride, he said it would open at five p.m.

At exactly five, buses started arriving outside the airport, and when hundreds of tourists disembarked, the airport filled up within minutes. All of them were White tourists from Toronto. We quietly joined their queue, and when they approached the immigration official, I quickly turned back and, in a valiant effort to change Sakunthala's expression into a joyous one, kissed her, who showed no sign of being startled. She stood silently. I handed over both our passports to the immigration official.

'What did you see in Santo Domingo?' the official asked. I gave him a prepared answer. Now the official turned to Sakunthala and started asking her questions. I could feel the sweat creeping down my spine like an ant. I thought it was over. Sakunthala's face returned to its natural state. Her expression contorted, as if she was going to sip a very hot coffee. That haunted look reappeared on her face. Her limbs began to tremble. She wasn't coherent. The young man who had spoken to us a couple of hours ago to tell us when the counter would open appeared in uniform now. He looked like the head of the immigration officials. He said something in Spanish and the official stamped both our passports. How true it is that sometimes God assumes the form of human beings.

It was well past midnight when we landed in Toronto. I told Sakunthala on the flight that after landing we were strangers.

'Don't turn and look at me. Neither will I, you. Remember yours is a fake Canadian passport. If you are caught, they won't send you back. You will be placed under detention. Just answer the questions they ask. You are coming back from a holiday in Santo Domingo. Show them the Toronto – Santo Domingo tickets. However tough the question is, don't panic and don't look at me.'

I stood before the immigration official. After a couple of questions, the official asked to examine my suitcase. I agreed. A Black female officer opened the suitcase and checked the contents. She took out the book titled *Kallukkul Eeram*.

'Hmm, a good cover,' she said. 'Are you carrying any liquor or cigarettes?'

I responded in the negative. The official proceeded to search, choosing not to trust me.

'How will you go home?'

'I will take a cab.'

The woman said 'thank you' and smiled. When she closed the suitcase, Canada's big doors opened for me.

The journey that had begun in Colombo in 1992 came to an end on a Friday on 10th October 1997. Columbus, who discovered America, had journeyed for seventy-one days. Marco Polo took three years and six months to travel to China. I took five years and two months.

Out of the corner of my eye, I saw that Sakunthala's bag was being examined by another official. Even from a distance, I could see Sakunthala's hands trembling. The officer opened a book from which a photo popped out.

'Who's this?' the official asked.

'My husband.'

'Where is he?'

'Germany.'

'What is he doing there?'

'He's in jail.'

She was speaking the truth without realising it. Her fake passport was in the official's hands. I was trembling now. She had lied to me that her husband was on business in India. Now she would be taken to a Canadian jail. Her husband was in a jail in Germany.

What could anyone do, I thought. Whatever I did, it would only make things worse. All the hard work had gone to waste. I remembered how she had risen early to learn to pronounce Mississauga. Two officials took her away. My eyes filled up with tears. Her figure moved hazily in my vision in the seven rainbow colours. Her two children would be waiting outside the airport.

I thought she would turn back to look at me.

But she did not.

She kept her promise.

SIXTEEN

Placeholder

As a child, I often visited the market with my mother, and while crossing the road with her, never looked to either side of the road. I would only look at my Amma's feet, follow them, and cross the road successfully. I trusted my mother so much.

When I landed in Canada, the first person I met was Nathan. I placed the same faith in him as I had in my mother, and spent two long years with him in a two-room house. My meeting him at the airport was the beginning of two completely wasted years in my stay in that country.

If my sister had been in Canada, none of this would have happened. She had introduced me to Nathan and relocated after her husband found a job in Dubai. I moved in with Nathan but did not know that I would be virtually enslaved. I had never met anyone as eccentric as Nathan. In winter, he would wear several layers of clothing and over them an overcoat, thus becoming so huge that nobody could hold him in an embrace. Once he returned home and removed his clothes, he would shrink to half the size, loll on the large sofa, and watch the weather channel continuously.

I had no idea how that information benefitted him. I realised that it was possible for someone to live in an utterly messy and chaotic house. Nathan would remove his clothes and throw them on the floor. The next day, he would pick them up, slip into them and leave. The room would be full of new bedsheets, blankets and towels. Everything in the house bore the logo of some hotel and were obviously stolen. These items included cups, ladles and even glasses. 'We spend so much in hotels, let them be our souvenirs,' he would boast. On the second day of my arrival, Nathan told me, 'Friend, you shouldn't think too much in this country. Stay with me and I'll teach you everything. Everything is easy in Canada. You shouldn't be worried about White people; their IQ is far below ours. We can easily understand subtle issues.'

I cleaned the house, washed the clothes and dried them, cooked and did other household chores every night without any coaxing from Nathan. He would open a bottle of Remy Martin saying '81 dollars' and pour our drinks. We would eat seated opposite to each other at the dining table, after which I washed the plates before retiring for the night.

After a week, I noticed that Nathan was not going to work. Like a lizard unable to move after a full meal, he slept all day on his stomach. When awake, he would watch the weather channels. If he received a phone call, he would attend to it in bed. At five in the evening, he would leave home after removing his lungi by slipping it over his shoulders and head and letting it drop on the floor in a circle. Returning home, he would stand in the centre of this circle and pull up the lungi to his waist.

I began to think that Nathan worked the night shift somewhere. He'd return after midnight with a bundle of new clothes, like T-shirts, pants, belts, socks, etc. I kept asking Nathan to get me a job, but he didn't show any interest. Wringing his hands as though he was wringing out wet clothes, he asked me to stay as his 'assistant'.

Why did he need an assistant? Did he want me to be his permanent cook? I could not understand him. If I did not have a job, how was I to pay the lawyer who was handling my asylum case.

Late one night, Nathan came home drunk. I hastily changed the channel I was watching to the weather. When he removed his overcoat, a number of credit cards dropped from it. Without picking them up, Nathan groped in his pockets and drew out four Canadian passports. I stood up.

'Look! Are you looking for work? All these are for you. I will teach you. You can run a huge business with me. Be ready to accompany me tomorrow,' mumbled Nathan and fell asleep in his overcoat.

Nathan did not believe in overusing his brain and operated at a different level. Though he appeared to be lethargic and sleeping continuously or speaking on the phone, deep down in his mind, he was constantly devising crooked plans. The next day, he wore an overcoat with large round buttons and took me to a supermarket.

'You don't have to do anything, don't come near me. Just watch me from a distance.'

I did just that.

Nathan entered the supermarket and selected two shirts. Including taxes, both cost ninety-four dollars. He paid with his fake credit card and signed. His purchases were always below a hundred dollars. He would have to produce his identity card if he bought anything above it.

My first new shirt in Canada was thus a stolen one. Once we had collected fifty or sixty shirts, Nathan would sell them. After a card ran dry, he would shred it before discarding it.

'How do you get the cards?'

'There are agents who take care of that,' responded Nathan.

The next day's training was at an ATM machine. Nathan took me at around 11.50 p.m., and at exactly 11.58 p.m., inserted a card, entered the pin and withdrew 400 dollars. At 11.59 p.m., I inserted another card and withdrew another 400 dollars. After midnight, when a new day was born, Nathan inserted his card for a second time and sought to withdraw 400 dollars. The machine refused to pay. When I tried my card, I got another 400 dollars. The 800 dollars were mine.

'We shouldn't be greedy. Your first try must be for 400 dollars. Sometimes we might get another 400, and sometimes not. After that, the card must be destroyed.'

I wondered if it was that easy. Thus began my new life.

Two years passed this way. Nathan expanded his business of using fake credit and debit cards and defrauding customers. I realised that Nathan was careful about never leaving any trace and made sure that if caught, all evidence pointed towards me. I would be the culprit if the police nabbed us some day and Nathan would surely go scot-free. Summoning up courage, I once asked Nathan about it.

'Well, the rider sits atop the horse.'

I was furious. Was I a horse? Holding my breath, I prepared a long response, but Nathan had disappeared by then.

Nathan treated me worse than he would a slave. He would rebuke me if the shirts did not fetch a good price. One day he screamed as if he was shouting at his wife, because I did not cook a good meal. There was no limit to his meanness.

One day, seated outside the supermarket, I reflected on my life. It had been months since I had spoken to my mother or even written to her. 'The butcher's clothes carry blood,' she would often say. I had accumulated a lot of blood in my life. Was it for this that I struggled so hard to reach Canada? Had I not reformed many people during my journey by lending them a sympathetic ear?

In Germany, Sathyan's application for asylum had been approved. He had married Sameera and they were both now working in a computer company. I felt proud when thinking of Jayakaran. The world belonged to him and nobody could do anything to unmake him. Suddenly I thought of Sakunthala. Where was she now? She might have been released or sent back. My stomach churned when I thought of how she had woken up early in the morning to learn the pronunciation of Mississauga. How hard she had struggled to be united with her children. She had even endured my surprise kiss.

'Friend!' I heard someone call out to me. It was a familiar voice. Shocked, I looked up. I couldn't believe that it was Kanakalingam the surveyor from Paris. My first sight of him in Canada was impressive—he was wearing boots, gloves and a thick overcoat. Like someone who had stood first in a hundred metre race, Kanakalingam was smiling, broadly. He hugged me so tight I couldn't breathe for some moments.

'Friend, when did you arrive? What are you doing these days?'

'I am working in a credit card company,' I said and hung my head. I couldn't look Kanakalingam in the eye.

We discussed old times over coffee. 'Have you built a stone house for your sister?' I asked, smiling, but soon realised I shouldn't have asked him that. Kanakalingam was not the man I had once known. He was wearing clean, neatly ironed clothes. He wore a long scarf and an expensive-looking watch. His hair was trimmed. Like a glass of water poured into a pond, he was now a part of the Canadian population. He inspired respect. He was no longer the Kanakalingam who had once begged for a peg of vodka.

'Friend, you did not forget me. It is because of your advice that I am here. Otherwise, I would have been lost.'

'You said you would play the nadaswaram in temples.'

'I said idiotic things in France. The truth is, there are a thousand ways to lead an honest life in a place like Canada. But you will have to give it a try. Nobody else can do it for you.'

'So what is it you do?'

'Friend, I am a placeholder. I wake up at five in the morning and stand outside embassies, holding ten passports. My job is to get numbers allotted to its owners. So, avoiding standing in a long queue at unearthly hours, they arrive at ten in the morning. I earn ten dollars for every passport. I stay at my son's place ... what else do I need?'

'What about your sister and her children?'

'I couldn't build them a stone house, but they are now staying in a rented house. The roof is taller than they are and doesn't bang their heads. The house has a door with a number on it. The rains don't enter the house like before. There is no mosquito menace in the night nor are there flies by day. Since they don't think about hunger all the time, the children are able to study well.'

'You are a man of action. I am proud of you.'

'We are lucky to have got into Canada. My life won't return to its old ways. Will a worm that has grown wings go back to crawling again? All we need is to be honest now. You will scale greater heights in the credit card company. I am old, I do whatever I can.'

'I will work hard to be as successful as you are.'

'What does success mean, my friend? The crow wins one day, the statue, another day.'

It felt as if someone had slapped me. I was ashamed and humiliated at the same time. In Paris, Kanakalingam had been like a child. Here, he was giving me advice. How responsible he had become! I thought about myself. Would my mother be proud of me? What would my sister think? How did I become what I had? I sat alone and downed two or three beers. Cars raced each other on the road. Then I crossed the road when the traffic lights signalled not to cross. An acrid liquid rose from my stomach and reached my mouth. All the vehicles speeded up, zig-zagging and avoiding me. My time had not yet come.

I pondered over Kanakalingam's words. It would be wise to stand on my own two feet.

I joined a restaurant. Nathan did not like it. He felt worse when I left the house to live by myself. He tried his best to draw me back to him. In the beginning, he tried to convince me, even begged. Then he started to threaten me. 'I will inform the police about you,' Nathan said.

'Do as you please, I will tell them how I was tricked into this situation.'

'I tell you, one day you will regret this. You will fall at my feet and beg for forgiveness. I won't take you back then,' Nathan said.

Thoughts of Kanakalingam stiffened my bones.

My refugee application case was dragging on. The lawyer couldn't comprehend what the stumbling block was. One day I received a letter from CSIS, Canadian Intelligence Service, asking me to appear for an interview. I was petrified. Perhaps, they had discovered my credit card or debit card frauds. Could I be forgiven, or would I be sent to jail? I wasn't sure. For a moment, I wondered if I should seek Nathan's help. But then, I decided against it.

I attended the enquiry. For an hour, the official grilled me about my refugee status. I repeated the answers I had given in court. When the enquiry was nearing its end, the official asked me, 'Do you have any enemies here?'

I was taken aback by the question. 'I need to have friends first. Only then can I have enemies. I don't even have friends yet.'

The official placed a file before me. It contained anonymous letters of various complaints against me. They claimed I wasn't from Sri Lanka, and that I was leading a comfortable life in Europe and had immigrated illegally to Canada. The letters were a mix of capital and small letters. Nathan's style! I had no doubt. The official smiled and wished me good luck.

I hadn't expected Nathan to go to such lengths to settle his scores with me. Nathan did not like me working and becoming independent. He expected me to remain a slave whereas I had seen how someone as naïve as Kanakalingam could build a new life in Canada. I was certain my request to be granted refugee status would be rejected. I wondered what to do next. But I forgot that fate is always ahead of us and does the unexpected.

SEVENTEEN

Plates

There was another Tamil at the Italian restaurant where I worked. He felt that Sri Lankan Tamils were washing plates the world over. His name was Saba and he wouldn't look up or speak. Around thirty-five or thirty-six years of age, he would stand for hours on end washing the plates. It was amusing to watch him clean the plates: he would bend backwards and make a great effort with every plate that reached him.

If someone tried to start a conversation with him then, Saba would cut them off with monosyllabic responses.

'Friend,' I said once, 'I am young and I wash plates, and I suppose it's fair that I do. But you came to Canada several years ago. I'm surprised you are still at it. Why?'

Saba looked at me from the corner of his eye. His hands did not stop working. Something like a smile appeared on his lips. Surprisingly, he started talking. 'Reason? The reason is one mark. If I had got one more mark, my life would have been entirely different. Who thought things would change so drastically? You joined this place two months ago. I have been working here for fifteen years, standing in the same spot and rinsing plates. This restaurant used to be small back then, owned by this same Italian proprietor. There was no conveyor belt in the old days as we have now. There were no machines. I wore gloves and washed all the plates.'

'Where is your village?'

'I studied in Nelliyadi Central Mahavidyalaya. I stood first in all the classes and Kulasekaram came second. The competition was between us. If I scored ninety-eight marks, my father asked me about the missing two marks. He probably thought I had left them behind in school. On annual day events, I would go on stage and return with all the prizes. It would be difficult to measure the happiness on my father's face. He worked as a driver in Manthikai Hospital. The next day, he would take me to the hospital and introduce me to all the doctors, speaking very proudly about me—so embarrassing!

'At the O level examination that was held simultaneously across Sri Lanka, I scored the highest marks in all subjects except one. The next day, it was Kulasekaram's photograph that was printed prominently on the front page of *Virakesari*. He had stood first in the Northern district. He had scored an extra mark in the total, and the paper had published a report praising him. There was not a single word about me, who had stood second. My father was very disappointed, he couldn't bear it. He did not go to work that day but roamed the streets. I realised what a huge humiliation it must have been for him.

'Kulasekaram went to Colombo for higher studies. My father decided to make up for this setback. I knew what was running through my father's mind; it was as visible as an egg in a lizard's stomach. My mother and sister were shocked at what he said.

'"Go to Canada," he said. "Study medicine there and come back as a doctor. You must prove your worth. Nobody appreciates you here." My mother started crying. My knees were trembling. My skinny sister grabbed my study table and started arranging her books on it.

'At that time, the going rate for Canada was eighty thousand rupees. My father took a loan at a huge interest rate and paid the agent. I set off from Colombo in 1984, the year Indira Gandhi was assassinated. I turned eighteen in the same month. For the first time, I saw my father's eyes brimming when we reached the Katunayake airport. He was driven mad because of my failure to obtain one more mark.'

'Which route did you take?' I asked.

'Like all others, I came via East Berlin, West Berlin, Spain and Mexico to Canada. When the plane landed in Montreal to refuel, I went to the immigration official exactly as instructed by the agent and requested refugee status. He accepted my application. The flight captain was mad as he had to pay a fine of 1500 dollars for flying me in without a visa. I stepped into Canada on a chilly day in November, wearing a flimsy shirt and cheap Bata shoes.

'There was no one to help me. All I owned were ten words in English, hardly sufficient in my hunt for a job. I landed this job of washing plates and agreed immediately because for this you don't need to know any language. I could converse in any language with the plates, working till eleven p.m. every day.

'The owner took a liking to me. I was his only Tamil employee. I learnt about different types of plates. The salad plate was large, the soup plate deep, and the food plate flat-edged and rimmed with gold. The smaller ones were side plates. Besides these, coffee and tea cups and wine glasses came to me for rinsing. I would fondly touch and clean them.

'I was reminded of my home when washing the plates and would start weeping. Some vessels were so heavy I couldn't even lift them. I had to wear gloves and scrub them hard before rinsing them off. At barely nineteen, I worked way harder than I was supposed to.

'A lot of refugees were arriving in those days, and I found jobs for all of them. I made new friends. My life filled up with feasts, entertainment, celebrations and bars.'

'But you came here to study medicine,' I intervened.

'Listen to my story, I am coming to that. I experienced independence for the first time in my life when I got here. I was on my own. I didn't have to seek anybody's permission. I was getting good money. I was celebrating life with friends. Our day would begin after the restaurant closed! We enjoyed ourselves till two or three a.m. Those were happy days.

'I forgot to tell you something. I had a girlfriend called Vandana in my village. She was the most beautiful girl in the village, poised and vibrant, like a tightly strung veena. She was sixteen and was my sister's classmate. She visited my home often, restlessly roaming around like a bee. She truly loved me and I, in turn, promised never to forget her. After arriving in Canada, I responded immediately to her first letter. To the second letter, I responded two weeks later. Then, I started ignoring her. I developed a friendship with a girl who was a regular visitor at the restaurant and even exchanged rings with her. Then, it broke.'

'The ring?'

'Are you stupid? The relationship. That was when my friends suggested I start a chit fund. "You are well respected," they told me. It was something that was going to change my life. I agreed and started two chit funds; fifty people joined, all of them refugees. The first draw was in my favour and I had $24,000 in hand, an unimaginable amount. My friends asked me to buy a car. I bought a brand new Chevrolet Nova for $18,000. A twenty-year-old refugee buying a new car in Canada was something historic.

'Along with the new car came new friends. Days passed and I continued to enjoy myself. My mind believed that this kind of life would never end. It was like an ant thinking that it had achieved independence after growing wings, hardly realising that the wings would be its death. I roamed around with my friends in my car. This way, I completed three years in Canada.

'One day I got a letter from my father. "Your friend Kulasekaram is studying medicine. When are you going to become a doctor?" The next day, I sobered up and looked through my accounts. I had to pay 15,000 dollars towards the chit loan. I started another chit to save my name. I took money from the new chit and repaid the old loan. It was like opening a new pit to close the old one. I was losing myself in debts. I sold my car. My debtors started pressurising me and their persistent phone calls irritated me. I couldn't sleep.

'One night, I moved to another location. Some people came to the restaurant and troubled the owner. Things were getting out of hand. At this point, I made the second decision that changed my life.

'It was 1988. My refugee application was approved and I had obtained permanent residence. I could travel anywhere in the world.

'"Go to India once and come back with a parcel. All your problems will be sorted out," a friend said. I couldn't solve my problems just by washing plates! My friend took responsibility for the trip. The persons concerned took care of my tickets and the money to buy stuff. Once I handed over the parcel to them, I would be paid 50,000 dollars. My problems would be at an end. A woman came and met me at a small restaurant in Bombay. She was as white as half-baked pork, with a shrew-like face. She refused to meet my eye and looked at my feet instead while we spoke. When I gave her 20,000 Indian rupees, she murmured that the stuff would come and left without looking back. I waited. Soon, heroin stuffed in two plastic bags and two large suitcases arrived. The man who brought them was thin and looked like someone who worked in a teashop. His actions were stupefying. He started his work with the ease of doing something he had done at least a thousand times before. Using a sharp knife, he completely removed the inner part of one suitcase. There were only the remains of the suitcase now. He took the next suitcase and removed its external casing. When he inserted the inner part of the first suitcase into the outer casing of the second one, it fitted perfectly. The plastic bags were thrust into the gap between the two walls and the gap was sealed with a special gum. It was now a new suitcase. Nobody would guess that it had drugs packed inside it.

'I landed in Toronto, rented a cab, drove it myself and reached my friend's place. He was ready. I took him along and went to the house on Lawrence Street in Port Union. That was the address I had been given. My friend cut open the suitcase, took the stuff out, put it in a plastic bag and went to the second floor. When he returned after some time, he was carrying 50,000 dollars. When I touched the money, I was ecstatic. I left in the car, and while driving I realised that there was no limit to the happiness a conspiracy could bring. My mind was devising new plans when suddenly, three police cars with sirens blaring and blue-red lights flashing, surrounded my car. One vehicle was in the front, one in the back and another on the side. I couldn't figure out how and from where they had arrived.

'Two policemen jumped out of the car on the side, pointing their guns and shouting at the top of their voices. "Where is the money? Where is the money?" they screamed. I did what I had learnt from watching many Hollywood films: I took out forty dollars from my wallet and offered it to them. But they grabbed the bundle of 50,000 dollars, handcuffed me and took me away. For all the effort on my part, I had the pleasure of touching the 50,000-dollar bundle only for forty seconds. Everything happened in the blink of an eye.

'Another shock awaited me the next day. The *Toronto Star* published a news report: "Jailbreak attempt sabotaged. Shanmugam Sabanathan arrested. Drugs worth 7.5 million dollars confiscated". How was I connected to the jailbreak? Very slowly, I understood the truth. The drugs bought for a mere 20,000 rupees in Bombay had a street value of 7.5 million dollars in Toronto. The mafia in jail wanted a naïve person to transport the drugs. I was that idiot. And then, I was given 50,000 dollars for smuggling drugs worth millions of dollars. The mafia needed this amount to break jail. But the police had tapped their phones and were waiting for my arrival. We all fell right into their trap.'

'How did the case end, brother?'

'Patience! I'm coming to that. I was sentenced to seven years' rigorous imprisonment at a maximum security prison. I was sent to Millhaven Institution in Kingston. Each cell had two people. When my inmate met me, he said, "My name is Martin, you can sleep in the bunk above." He did not speak much. He had a tattoo of a skull on his chest. He was a tall, dark man and looked like a basketball player. He instantly reminded one of a bison. Months later, I learnt that he had murdered a school girl.

'The room had a TV and a radio installed in the wall. There was no mirror. A shining metal plate was fixed above the water tap. If I did something he didn't like, Martin would growl. I would stop whatever I was doing. There was a square-shaped hole in the door of our cell. All the meals came through this hole on a metal plate. If I didn't eat my meal immediately, Martin would have it.

'My stomach woke up five minutes before I did. I understood the meaning of hunger. It's a bad thing. Hunger doesn't even have an antonym. Have you ever thought about it?

'"Sleep, it isn't going to harm your eyes," Martin would say after breakfast.

'One day, Martin tuned into the radio. When changing stations, suddenly a Tamil song came streaming on the airwave. I ran to the radio. An ordinary song left me deeply troubled.

Paadatha paatellaam paada vanthaal
Kaanatha kangalai kaana vanthaal
Pesatha mozhi ellam pesa vanthaal.
Pen paavai nenjile aada vanthaal

She came to sing the songs that were not sung before.
She came to see the eyes she'd not seen before.
She came to speak the language that wasn't spoken before.
The young damsel came to dance in my heart.

'Martin immediately changed the radio station. Several thousand miles apart, in a dark cell in the Kingston maximum security prison in Canada, I heard a Tamil song. It was Vandana's favourite song. She would keep humming it.

'I can't explain in words the kind of emotions the song triggered in me on that day. The song played for exactly forty seconds. That wretched Martin spoilt everything I enjoyed.

The entire day, she was dancing in my heart. Why did I reject her? Would she be thinking of me at this moment when my heart was remembering her?

'A rat often came to our cell. Martin's body shrank like a damp cloth and trembled like a four-year-old kid. He would stand behind me and shout at me in a panic to catch it. To catch a rat, one has to think like a rat. To catch a buffalo, it is enough to think like you—I wanted to tell him but never did.

'Martin wasn't really so bad. As the days passed by, I took a liking to him. Before going to sleep every night, he would go down on his knees for a while.

'"What are you doing?" I would ask.

'"I am talking to the master of this world," he would say.

'I couldn't believe that he had killed an innocent girl. When I was released after four years because of my good conduct, it was difficult to say goodbye to him. When I took leave of him, he called me by my name "Saba" for the first time. Beyond that, he couldn't say anything.'

'What did you do after coming out?'

'What could I do? For four years, life had meant only sounds. The sound of iron gates being locked, the sound of guards barking instructions, the sound of boots, the sound of plates clanking, the sound of inmates screaming.

'Outside, the world was peaceful. My friends had disappeared. Even my shadow appeared to dislike me. But my Italian employer remembered me, and the plates were waiting for me. For four years, I had seen only metal plates. Seeing ceramic plates at the restaurant, I was happy beyond words.

'"I will start tomorrow," I told the owner.

'"Will your brain power double by tomorrow? Start now," he said.

'I have washed two million plates till now to repay my loan.'

'Brother, couldn't you have found another job?'

'Why? The whale will weigh the same even if it's dead. A man is not shocked by anything after he reaches the age of thirty-five. Kulasekaram, with whom I competed in school, is now a neurologist in London. He is among the top ten neurologists in the world. I am almost the same. If you make a list of the top ten plate washing experts in the world, I would top that list, having washed over two million plates.'

'Do you regret anything?'

'What kind of question is this? I have accepted my fate. What we consider the end is actually a beginning. Truth assumes the role of a widow; falsehood adorns itself in wedding attire. The day after the police caught me, *Veerakesari*, the Tamil daily, carried my photograph and published this: "Sri Lankan Tamil Shanmugam Sabanathan's jailbreak attempt fails. Drugs worth 7.5 million dollars seized." How my father must have suffered! How deeply he would have been pained to know that his son who left for Canada after losing a single mark to do medicine had ended up like this. I learnt that he couldn't believe the news and had roamed the streets, carrying the newspaper and crying aloud the name he used to call me by when I was a child: "Sabu kutti! Sabu kutti!"

'I never got the opportunity to apologise to him or offer him some solace. He was dead in two months.'

Soup, salad, side and dinner plates arrived with precision on the conveyor belt.

I picked up a soup plate.

Saba picked a salad plate.

Hundreds of plates were in line, waiting their turn.

EIGHTEEN

The Miracle of Milk

For several days afterwards, I wondered if I was chasing fate or fate, I. However much I planned, something entirely unforeseen always overtook me. A completely unanticipated event occurred at a totally unexpected time. But everything happened with some kind of precision. One event touched the other, which in turn linked with another. Life moved forward like a giant relay race. Throughout the world, when there are those who eat, there will be work for those who wash plates. I continued to work at the restaurant in Canada like I had in Germany, but I couldn't stand for twelve hours on end like Saba and wash plates. My feet ached. I was willing to do any job other than washing plates.

Suddenly, Kalpatharu Vilas, a famous restaurant in Toronto, offered me a job. My work was to sit at the reception counter, collect money from the customers and keep accounts. Irrespective of the restaurants I worked in, I would always find someone to chat to.

'Aachi, how did you come to Canada? Where is your husband? You say you are living alone.'

Aachi worked in the kitchen. She made puttu and mothakams. She also made sambal for idiyappams.

'Thambi, you are also calling me Aachi? You have just joined this place, right?'

'That's what everybody calls you. I can call you Amma too.'

'It's all right, call me Aachi ... Can you guess my age?'

I looked at her. Her hair was white as snow, there was nothing left to turn white on her head. I said she could be sixty-five. 'Thambi, I have just turned fifty. Everybody is deceived by my hair.'

I looked closely at her unwrinkled face. 'You don't have anybody here ... How did you reach Canada?'

'I have no husband or children now. But I have never been alone. I had my parents. I had a husband, and a child. I was a mother for an hour—my baby died an hour after it was born.'

'Where is your native place, Aachi?'

'Thellipalai. Don't take me to be an illiterate. I scored three As in the A level exam and I got admission into a university too. But my father got me married. My husband was working in the income tax department. Then—well, you know all about what happened. The civil war. My husband and I decided to leave the country. He sent me off to Canada with a relative saying he would join me in six months after sorting out the pension issues.'

A customer came to buy twenty vaipans. I attended to him, and after he had left, asked, 'Did you come through an agent?'

'Yes, Thambi, we paid him by selling our land. He was a very capable agent. I was forty at the time and the boy who brought me was seventeen. His name was Aravindan. He held his tickets tightly, like a schoolgirl holding her knitting kit. Throughout the journey, I had to take care of him. He understood something only after I repeated it many times. He was timid. The agent brought us uptill Germany through Russia. We encountered no problem until then. Next was to travel to Canada from Germany. There, we faced a major problem.

'We travelled on Sri Lankan passports. Getting fake passports would have meant huge expenses. Since Ecuador in South America did not call for visas, the agent bought tickets to Ecuador for us. We had to fly from Frankfurt. Though we got our boarding passes, we were told that the German immigration was a tough one to pass through, and they would grill us. A Tamil gentleman named Arumugam, who was a sanitation worker in the Frankfurt airport, took us to the basement in the service elevator that is not accessible to passengers. In the basement, he gave us the uniforms of sanitation workers and led us to the upper floor by another elevator where he retrieved the uniforms and sent us on our way. We had now bypassed the immigration. Arumugam did not take a single cent! I think God appeared to us in his form.

'We faced no problem in Ecuador. We travelled to Panama from there and stayed at Sole Hotel as arranged by the agent. We could do nothing there but wait till the Panama agent got in touch with us.

'Then something unusual happened. Some Indians who were staying in the hotel were visited by some others from different countries. They held animated discussions and left quickly. It was all very mysterious! When I made enquiries, I was told that the idols of Pillaiyar in temples all over the world were drinking milk offered by devotees. I couldn't believe it. The Gujaratis living in Panama had constructed a Vishnu temple on a hill, and the miracle was happening there too.'

I received an order over the phone for Thali meals for twenty people. I made a note of it and asked Aachi, 'What happened afterwards?'

'I asked Aravindan if we could go to the temple and he refused. He was upset after receiving a phone call from the agent in the morning. He refused to engage in any conversation with me.

'"Canada isn't going to run away. We can't be certain that a miracle like this will ever find us again. Either you come to the temple or I will go alone," I threatened him and he agreed to come. We travelled for an hour by cab to the hill temple.

'We couldn't help being stunned by the temple. Panama is a small country, located between the Pacific Ocean and the Atlantic Ocean. The Gujaratis who had travelled ten thousand miles away from their homes to settle there had built a magnificent temple. The marble floor and the temple tower were stunning. Indians, White people, Black people, all were standing in a long queue. When it was my turn, I offered three spoons of milk to the idol and it was sucked into thin air. Aravindan called it an act of folly and refused to participate.

'Once we got back to the hotel, the agent came and took us away. We crossed several borders—I don't remember their names. Finally, we were handed over to a Mexican in Mexico. He was frightening and looked as if he was ready to chew something. When he spoke, it sounded like a snake hissing. He put us up in an old building where there were eighteen others, including Indians, Africans and Mexicans. Only two of them were Sri Lankans. Aravindan was horrified. "Pillaiyar is exacting revenge, Akka. I am going to die," he said. Suddenly, the Mexican came and urged us to leave. The auspicious moment we were waiting for had arrived.

'Each of us was handed a black plastic bag in which were placed a litre of milk, a litre of water, two loaves of bread and four bananas. As instructed, we wrapped the bags around our waists. That was going to be our sustenance for the next two days. We could not discard garbage on the way. We had to save it in the bags we carried.

'It was night-time. The Rio Grande river flowed between Mexico and America. Having flowed for two thousand miles, the river had grown tired and was now only waist-deep. We were in Matamoras city. If we crossed the river, we would reach Brownsville, a city in America. We stepped into the river and started crossing it once we received a signal from the Mexican agent. A bloated white corpse floated by, almost striking us. Nobody showed any emotion.

'In the middle of the river, Aravindan said, "Akka, forgive me, I have betrayed you." I couldn't understand what he meant.

'There was a dense forest on the other side of the river. This was the worst part. We had to walk for an entire day through it. The American border patrol was on their rounds; if caught, we would immediately be jailed. All of a sudden, an Indian travelling with us had an epileptic seizure. He couldn't take another step. The entire group was at the risk of being caught, because he kept collapsing. The Mexican agent made a unilateral decision, without consulting anyone. There were wheel tracks made by vehicles when the border patrol made their rounds. The man was laid along the depression in the dirt track. His passport, documents and bag were seized. He was left there, with a bottle of water and bananas. He pleaded and screamed not to be left behind. He cried out something in his mother tongue. His miserable voice followed us for a long time in the woods.

'"You are now on American soil. In two hours, the American border patrol will rescue him. He will get first-class treatment. If the coyotes spare him, he will secure citizenship before most of you," said the Mexican agent.

'I will never forget how we abandoned him. How pitious he looked when we left him behind, howling! I can still hear his cries. It was then that I realised the real value of life. The value of life changes from country to country. A country's development cannot be measured by its space programme or by its nuclear weapons. Not even by the number of rich people in it. It is measured by the value it attaches to a life, not just human life.

'A few days ago, in Canada, when I was travelling by a bus, a moose darted from the wild into the road. It was bigger than a horse and had long antlers. There was fear in its eyes. Not the fear of seeing the bus, but the fear that its forest cover had disappeared and that the road had invaded the forest. However hard the driver tried to avoid it, the bus hit the animal. The moose lay on the road, its legs splayed in all directions. Its head did not touch the road but was held up by its antlers. The police arrived in a few minutes and stopped the traffic. An emergency vehicle rushed the moose to a veterinary hospital. The road came back to normalcy in the fifth minute. I was stunned by the importance given to the wild animal. I thought of the Indian we had left behind at the Rio Grande river in the deep tracks of a tyre.'

'What happened after that, Aachi?'

'We came to Buffalo from Texas, crossed the Canadian border and applied for refugee status. We had already torn our passports. Canada took us in without any problem. I prayed to the Panama Pillaiyar. But you won't believe what happened next. Aravindan, who was tagging along all this while, disappeared. As soon as I reached Canada, I called the agent in Germany. He conveyed his condolences to me.'

'"Condolences for what?" I asked.

'"Didn't Aravindan tell you?"

'"No."

'"Your husband passed away."

'"What! When?" I screamed.

'"When you were in Panama, I told Aravindan that I would arrange for your return journey to Colombo. Did he not tell you?"

'Thambi, when I was feeding milk to Pillaiyar, my husband was dead and lying in a mortuary in Colombo. This boy did not tell me. I had been imagining a life with my husband in Canada, but God had different plans.'

'Did you meet Aravindan again?'

'No, Thambi. He would have thought he did me a good turn. And perhaps it was all written in my destiny. I called Colombo and asked the Sinhala doctor what had happened to my husband and he just said he died without a struggle … I have been working in Kalpatharu Vilas for ten years, Thambi. I recite all slokas, *Devaram* and hymns. But I never sing the devotional poem on *Pillaiyar, "Paalum Thelithenum"*, because it has the word "milk" in it. I lose my peace of mind when I say the word milk.'

'Aachi, bearing so much agony and grief in your heart, how do you keep calm? Your face doesn't betray your pain.'

Aachi said, 'Thambi, if someone gives you a wet sari, can you wear it while it's damp? You don't have to do anything. Wait for a few hours and it will dry on its own. Then you can wear it. Our troubles are similar. We don't have to do anything. In time they will disappear on their own.'

As I was about to ask another question, our employer rushed in. Aachi suddenly started reciting the *Sahasranamam*, clearing her throat. I picked up the accounts book and opened page number 166.

NINETEEN

Any Bad News?

As a child, I often dreamt of angels granting me boons. As I grew older, I dreamt of winning millions in a lottery. On some days, I imagined being overwhelmed by an incredible stroke of luck. That afternoon, I struck it lucky in real life. Before I could recover from the first stroke of luck, another hit. Two strokes of luck in a single day!

I had been working at Kalpatharu Vilas on Kennedy Road in Toronto for two years now. The restaurant opened at ten in the morning and closed at ten in the night. It was a takeaway joint, with no dining facilities. Yet, customers would queue up to buy stuff. Indian and Sri Lankan delicacies, including vadai, vaaipan, idly, mothagam, rice and curries, were all sold in the restaurant, but puttu and idiyappam were the bestsellers.

Mine was a desk job, but sometimes I would assist in chopping vegetables in the kitchen when there were no customers. I also helped prepare the dough for idiyappam and clean the large pots and pans.

The cook would arrive daily at five in the morning and leave by noon. Aachi was his assistant. She would often say, 'Thambi, all that is left are my memories. But nowadays, I tend to lose them too.'

Sometimes Aachi would forget to carry out the owner's instructions. But worse was doing things she wasn't required to do. Which is what happened on that particular day. The owner reprimanded her and left.

Aachi wept.

'What did he say?'

'He did not like the shape of the vadai I made. He said it looked like a cow's mouth.'

The truth, though, was that he had referred to another part of the cow's anatomy. But Aachi was too embarrassed to say it.

'I am going to quit!'

Aachi had threatened to quit at least twenty times, but the problem was that three months' salary was always due to her.

'Work for one more month, and I will settle all the dues,' the owner would say. But that never happened.

For twenty days in a month, Aachi fasted. Her lips were forever chanting slokas. She knew the *Devaram* and *Thiruvasagam* by rote. Aachi's recitals had a mathematical precision to them. By the time the *Periya Puranam* was done, eight rounds of puttu would have been steamed. They had an electric machine for making idiyappam. By the time two hundred idiyappams were done, she would have finished reciting the *Kanda Sashti Kavasam*. Aachi worked tirelessly. Her house keys always hung from a chain around her neck. One day, she left mothagams frying and, chanting the *Karumari Amman* slokas, she started to cut the greens. The mothagams got overcooked to a black sludge and had to be discarded.

Aachi's request for refugee status ran into no problem. When quizzed, she would give all the credit to the translator who provided all the answers secretly when translating the questions into Tamil. Of course, the official wasn't aware of this—possibly a miracle of Panama's *Pillaiyar*.

Aachi particularly loathed the winter in Canada. She would weigh twice her normal weight in winter. Weighed down by three cardigans and an overcoat two sizes too big, she would arrive like a rolling drum. Her lips frozen, Aachi would never be able to utter the words she intended to speak.

She had rented a tiny flat in a quiet neighbourhood with the wages she earned. But for the restaurant owner's frequent reprimands, Aachi would be leading a contented life.

When Aachi arrived in the morning, a red cardinal with a crown on its head would come along chirping as if to welcome her. Aachi would wave and smile at the bird, enter the shop and ask me, 'Theengulavo?' (Any bad news?) She would never greet me with a hello or good morning. Her greeting was always an inquiry about negative news. According to her, it was always a good day if there was no bad news. This famous word 'Theengulavo' was spoken by Thilakavathiyar when she saw her saint brother Navukarasar returning to her after a long absence.

The restaurant had received an order for a hundred Thali meals, but as usual, Aachi, who had to cut twenty pounds of vegetables for the cook early the next day, forgot. It was a significant day—*Aavani Moolam*. The day when Lord Shiva, disguised as a young man, helped an old lady to fill the bund with sand in exchange for her puttu. He had to bear strikes from the Pandya king's cane because he had failed in his duty. In remembrance of that holy day, Aachi collected all the loose puttu that had dropped off the steamer and distributed them to the customers for free. 'Amma, for you, Aiya—have this. This is God's offering. You will not face any difficulties this whole year,' she said. Only when the owner turned up and yelled at her did she remember that she had forgotten to chop the onions.

The next day, Suguna joined us. She needed to earn enough to pay the lawyer who was handling her refugee application. After the refugee status was settled, she planned to study. To me, it appeared that she was not there to cook or to help in any way. She came dressed as if to a party. Breasts thrust out and alluring enough to stop a conversation, she wandered about like a lost mermaid. She had a word of advice for me on her very first day. 'Brother, you know nothing about marketing. I have studied it. A person who asks for mothakam shouldn't leave with just that. He should also buy some vadai. A person dropping in to buy a Thali meal should also take away a litre of payasam. That's the way to run a business. It isn't enough to just sit, collect money and drop it in the till.'

Ask her to chop onions and she would take an hour, as if she had been asked to measure the pieces for their symmetry. On day two, she started issuing orders to Aachi. On the fourth day, she was attending to the telephone calls she received continuously. What was surprising, though, was that the owner who was always on his cell phone and never present in the restaurant started dropping in often. He lingered in the kitchen to supervise. He was no ordinary man. If a coin fell to the floor, he could tell by the sound it made whether it was a one dollar or two dollar coin or a quarter. Except when filling the census form, he always had a wild imagination. He was constantly discovering new dishes. He was the first to create a dish called 'mithivedi' (landmine) in Canada. It was extremely hot and spicy.

Like a message landing silently in a mobile phone even when a hundred people are around, Suguna would slip away and stand next to the owner once he arrived. Like a loyal maid, she would crane forward and look him in the face, as if reading it. She would find a table, stand close as if pasted to it, and peel the potatoes. Aachi noted their hushed conversations, eye locks and signals. Yet she would continue reciting the *Vishnu Sahasranamam*.

Aachi was done with making mothakams for the day. 'If you bite into it, the mothakam should melt and let the juices flow,' she would say. That was the precise Thellipalai recipe. Idiyappams were counted in hundreds and stored in a rigifoam box. Aachi's style of counting was different. She counted in reverse order—like it's done at a rocket launch—100, 99, 98, and so on. Ask her why and she would say it was difficult to keep count in ascending order. Often, she would lose track and start counting all over again.

It was 11 a.m. and Suguna hadn't turned up. But before we could heave a sigh of relief, there she was, gracefully arching her neck and floating in like a moth drawn to light. Blue danglers danced on her ears. She was wearing a blue salwar suit and blue plastic bangles to match.

'It's my birthday today,' she declared. She was all decked up—her nails were glittering, her eyebrows enhanced, and she had worn an unusual shade of lipstick. Twirling on her heels, she dumped her bag in a corner. When the rest of us were wondering how she would dice vegetables or knead the dough for puttu in that attire, the owner arrived. She announced it was her birthday, as though he was unaware of it. When she bowed to receive his greeting, I thought she was about to throw up. The owner not only blessed her by placing his hands on her head, but also ordered a birthday cake with her name on it. I had had two birthdays and Aachi ten in his employment, but neither of us had seen a cake! For a woman who had joined just two weeks ago, a cake worth fifty dollars had been ordered. They first fed the cake to each other, and what remained would be distributed among us.

What happened next was even worse. The owner's wife arrived in a towering rage. It appeared that she was already familiar with Suguna. She looked for her husband but couldn't find him.

'Akka, have some cake,' Suguna offered.

'Never mind, where did you get these danglers?'

'From a shop.'

'Who gave them to you?'

'What's it to you?'

'Mine are missing. Give them back to me!'

The wife walked towards Suguna, arms outstretched. Two pairs of gold bangles adorned her wrists.

'Akka, look, you will lose your dignity. Stop! If you don't, your bangles will also be mine.'

After admitting that the earrings were not hers, Suguna stood like a rock.

'Leave! Get lost right away! Either you will stay here or I!' screamed the owner's wife.

'Okay, let me leave. I won't come back, unless the owner of Kalpatharu Vilas falls at my feet and begs me to return.' Suguna rushed out, picking up her handbag and swinging it.

Her birthday also left with her. Aachi somehow managed to pacify the wife and send her off.

The calliope hummingbird flaps its wings eighty times per second without making the slightest noise. Similarly, the owner's BMW was soundless. He stepped out of his car and banged the door before entering the restaurant. I buried my head in an accounting book, pretending to write something. Aachi was chopping eggplants. He trashed whatever Aachi had cut and said, 'Leave. It's because of you that all this has happened. Out!'

The second scene unfolded. For the first time, Aachi raised her voice. 'Cough up the three months' wages I'm owed, and I will leave right away.'

'Should I pay for the damages you have caused? I have incurred losses because of you.'

'What about my service all these years?'

'Service? Did you donate blood?'

'I asked for my dues. Did I ask for blood? Or did I trouble you for danglers?'

The owner jumped as if a pickle jar had been dropped on his foot. He was livid. Like an animal that gathers all its strength in its hindlegs, he stood up and charged towards her. Fearing an assault, Aachi ran but slipped and fell down on the steps. The owner left in a huff in his noiseless car.

I knew it wasn't wise to immediately help someone to their feet after a fall. It made things worse if there was a fracture. I bent over to ask her, 'What happened Aachi? Did you fall?' Even at that hour, Aachi's sense of humour was intact. 'I did not fall, Thambi. It's been a long time since I felt the roads. I just had a closer look.' Like the red colour splashed across the sky, Aachi's cardinal bird flew close by, chirping, and looked at

Aachi. Aachi did not take her eyes off the bird. An ambulance arrived, lights flashing. Despite the siren's sounds, the bird continued to chirp, and hovered until the ambulance left with Aachi. Then it flew off.

I was restless. A few customers came in. One of them asked for paniyaram made of palmyra fruit. When I said it was not available, the customer got angry.

'You call your restaurant "Kalpatharu", which means food is inexhaustible, and now you say you're out of stock?' he shouted.

I was about to lose my temper but explained that palmyra fruits were expected to arrive in a container next week and that I would send word when it became available. Just then, the telephone rang. My application for asylum had been accepted. My lawyer opened the letter and read its contents over the phone. I couldn't believe it.

'Read it once again,' I said.

How many times had I been turned away from the borders. I had been beaten with a cane; I had spent time in jail. I had lost three lovers. The good news came as if it were compensation for all the losses.

Aachi wasn't around to share the good news with. Happily, I distributed the leftover cake to the customers who walked in.

When the owner came back at 8 p.m., I left to see Aachi in the hospital. I was upset thinking of Aachi lying on the floor like an abandoned creature. She had done no wrong. The owner's anger was always directed at the poor. After boarding a bus, I tried hard to remember Aachi's real name. I simply could not recollect what it was. How would I look for her in the hospital?

One day, I had asked Aachi, 'Aachi, what is your name?'

'I have no clue, Thambi. Look at this card,' she said, handing over the card to me.

'How do you not know your name?' I asked, surprised.

'I came here after tearing up my passport, Thambi. I was given so many names en route. How many names could I remember? Everybody calls me Aachi. The other details are in the card.'

'But, Aachi, you would have had a name when you were born.'

'Oh, that? I was called Valliyammai. But the lawyer had told me that I shouldn't mention my name anywhere because I travelled on a fake passport.'

I remembered this conversation right when I got down from the bus and walked towards the hospital. After some searching, I found her by accident. Aachi smiled and asked, 'Theengulavo?'

'There is no bad news,' I told Aachi and handed over some apples to her. Aachi looked strange in the grey hospital gown. Her flesh was hanging like dewlaps from her arms. Her fingers were gnarled like ginger roots. I was moved looking at her. Aachi sounded optimistic though.

'The X-ray showed nothing wrong, Thambi. No bones broken. By the mercy of Panama *Pillaiyar,* I could go home tomorrow.'

'Good to hear that, Aachi. I was worried.'

'But I lost my job, Thambi. What will I do? I have no one to turn to.'

All the orifices on her face started to stream.

'Don't worry, Aachi. I will speak to the owner. It'll be difficult for him to find someone to replace you.'

'Thambi, the young witch will be back.'

'That won't happen. We will work together again. The restaurant will be under our control.'

But my prediction did not materialise. Aachi did continue to work at the restaurant. I, however, had to quit the job. A moment I could never have anticipated in all my life was waiting for me at the hospital reception.

TWENTY

Where God Began

As I was hurrying out, a little girl standing at the hospital reception called out—'Uncle! Uncle!' I continued to walk on. But the girl rushed towards me and held my hands. 'Uncle,' she said again. I didn't know who she was. She had a beautiful smile.

'I know you. Looks like you don't know me,' she said, and turning back, smiled with a tinge of pride. I bent down, patted her cheeks and asked, 'What do you need, little girl?' I still couldn't guess who she was.

A Tamil woman dressed in western clothes was seated behind her, smiling at me. I was unable to recognise who she was either. Then she rose and walked towards me. Glowing complexion, high heels that made sounds like fire igniting, she carried a handbag that probably cost more than my month's salary. Her hair though casually groomed was surely the handiwork of an expert hairdresser.

'Don't you recognise me? I am Eswari. We stayed together in the Ukraine apartment. She's Laila, my daughter.'

I gaped. Years fell away from the present, making way for memories. Standing at the hospital reception, we exchanged old stories. I briefly narrated mine. She listened to some of it in disbelief. When she recounted what had transpired after she landed in Canada, it was no less astonishing.

Handing me her business card, she said, 'I think of you often, you know ... you made a great change in my life. I have enquired about you from every Sri Lankan refugee I met here because I've been looking for someone as honest and as good-natured as you. Please meet me at your convenience,' and left holding her daughter's hand.

Was this the same Eswari? I remembered how Alex had wiped the sofa clean with his hands before she sat on it, like a queen.

I would call Ambikapathi Master whenever I was in serious trouble. Once, on contemplating suicide after much humiliation and pain, I had called him. At that time, I had realised I couldn't fall any lower in life. My request for refugee status was still in abeyance. Nathan had threatened to expose the lies in my application to the authorities if I so much as talked about leaving him or his job, and so, for two years I had had to suffer the ignominy of working like a slave.

'Master, those who came later than me have secured well-paying jobs and are leading good lives. I'm still living like a slave, bound to Nathan. Looks like this will not change for another twenty years. Why is this happening to me? To me and only me?'

I never forgot what Ambikapathi Master said that day. He told me the story of the American tennis player Arthur Ashe. In the '70s, Ashe had ranked first among the world tennis players. He had won the Wimbledon and was also a US Open and Australian Open champion. Tragically, in 1983 he got HIV AIDS through a blood transfusion during a bypass surgery.

'Why has God chosen *you* for such a cruel ailment?' a fan had asked him in a letter.

His response became world famous. 'Fifty million children started playing tennis, five million learnt to play tennis, five hundred thousand learnt professional tennis, fifty thousand came to the circuit, five thousand reached Grand Slam, fifty reached Wimbledon, four reached the semifinals, two reached the finals … And when I was holding the cup, I never asked God, "Why me?" So now that I'm in pain, how can I ask God, "Why me?"'

'Ashe said this. You know what, you are in the midst of bad times. This too shall pass. Good things will surely reach you. Have patience,' said Ambikapathi Master.

Now my application for asylum had been accepted. Eswari was offering me a job. I could start my life anew, like a teacher wiping the previous day's maths problems off the board and writing new ones.

All the way home on the bus, these thoughts crowded in my mind. I could not believe how the skin-and-bones Eswari had transformed into someone so attractive and elegant. The things she said and the way she said them were unique. After the incident in Ukraine, she had confessed to her husband and wept. He had spent a fortune and taken her to France. She studied in France for two years, and after that, the couple moved to Canada with their daughter. In Canada, her husband set up a business that exported its products to America.

Only one word echoed in my ears throughout the journey back to my room: honest. I would have barely spoken to Eswari when we stayed together in Ukraine. But she had been observing me and had concluded that I was honest. Would she still have the same opinion if she learned of my life in Canada?

Two days later, I went to the address Eswari had given me. Her office was in the centre of Toronto, on the fourteenth floor of a huge building. After studying the appearance of the woman at the reception, I looked at myself. Embarrassment and inadequacy swept over me. When I said I was there to meet Eswari, she asked me to be seated.

When I sat, the sofa sank half a foot. The entire office was sparkling as if someone was cleaning it every ten minutes. A pleasant scent filled the room; it was difficult to guess where it came from. Red and yellow tulips adorned a three-foot tall glass vase.

When asked to go in, I rose and walked. I stopped where the carpet stopped. Then summoning courage, I proceeded, knocked on the door, and waited for a response.

Eswari greeted me like she would an ambassador. The office, in pale green, was pleasing to the eye. The bookshelf was stacked with law books. Eswari was working. I sat still and relaxed, hiding the tension in my heart.

Suddenly she asked, 'Do you know the Thelon?'

'It's a river running through Canada.'

'The Thelon valley connects Canada's Yukon, the Northwest Province and the Northern Hemisphere. I've been there. The earth remains the same there, as it was in ancient times. The same trees, the same river, the same animals, the same birds, the same humans. If you are there, it is difficult to look away from the land.

'That land is called 'Where God Began'. The Inuit, the indigenous people of that region, believe God started Creation from there. That is why we decided to call our company "Thelon Export Company". Since we launched, the business has flourished. God's blessings are with us. We have opened a branch in Ottawa. I thought of you when we opened it. You might find it hard to believe, but that's the truth. We need someone like you who is honest and intelligent. You are capable of grasping intricate things. You should first learn how to manage this branch. Later, my husband will bring other aspects to your attention. It is important that you stay happy because you are responsible for what I am today. Thank you.' Her voice grew hoarse as she stopped.

When I caught the bus to Ottawa, I had not informed anyone. The appointment letter was in my bag. I wanted to call my mother first and share the good news with her. In Ottawa, I would stay in the company's guest house to begin with and then look for independent accommodation later. Eswari had told me that it was a managerial position, but given me no other details. I thought about all the paths I had crossed in my journey. So many countries, so many people ... This moment had to be treasured and remembered all my life.

Ambikapathi Master had told me about a Roman god named Janus. A two-headed God. One head faced forwards and the other backwards. One head looked at the past and the other at the future. A person has nothing called the present. The future is everything. And the future was in my hands now—I had to cherish it.

A cute white puppy lay in the lap of the woman seated next to me on the bus.

'It's beautiful. What breed is the pup?' I asked.

'This is not a pup; it is a Maltese. It remains the same size as an adult.'

We struck up a conversation. She was going to Ottawa for the first time to join a bank.

'Why did you choose Ottawa?' I asked.

'It's Canada's capital. I've also read that it is the cleanest city in the world and that people there are kind.'

Her eyes left me stunned. Elongated eyes, as if someone had carved them with a chisel. Her fingers disappeared into the dog's fur. I asked her name.

'Drupa,' she said. 'I like the second part of your name; in our language it means money. The first part, in my language, means warning,' she said.

What might her mother tongue be, I wondered.

Was she making fun of me?

When the bus reached the terminal, both of us were taken aback by the sight of a large tree there. The tree had lost all its leaves except for one.

'It isn't willing to let go of this last one,' I said.

'No, the *leaf* is pleading to not let it go,' she said.

'The leaf and the tree may have mutually decided not to spoil the cleanest city on the earth,' I replied.

We laughed.

I had been very close to Divya, Laura and Ahalya. But they had forgotten me almost immediately. Lovers were initially attracted but soon abandoned me. I had never understood why.

I thought of the high-caste Pushpanathan and Keyar.

Someone had been killed over a fish.

I remembered Sathyan, Sameera, Masi and the refugee magistrate.

How could I forget Saba of the Italian restaurant, stone house Kanakalingam and Sakunthala?

Together, they had created me.

When I got down from the bus and started walking, my thoughts skipped. Drupa was stunning. If I thought of something, she spoke about it almost instantly, as if reading my mind. She had taken my mobile number. Would she ever call me?

A man sped past on a bicycle, almost hitting me. I wasn't irritated. It was as if someone had filled my body with air. The sky shone blue. Small white clouds moved together in one direction.

I started looking for directions on my new cell phone. Two young girls were seated closely in a park, sharing a pair of earphones to listen to music. I felt happy seeing them.

I said 'hi' to them. They responded with a 'hi'.

It got dark by the time I reached my street.

I looked at every door.

On a large door made of oak wood, the name Thelon Export Company was clearly visible in the light from the street-lamps. I had never seen such a smooth marvel of a door. I reached for the keys Eswari had given me.

On that night, when the lights were shining brightly, I directed the keys towards the keyhole in the door.

My future was waiting on the other side.

Suddenly, there was a power cut and darkness engulfed me. I was shocked but only slightly—it was probably a regular outage. But that wasn't the case. It was a historic power cut that was going to impact ten million people in Canada and forty-five million people in the USA for two full days.

It was Thursday, 14 August 2003.

The next day, the international media would write about the sweeping power failure.

I couldn't see the key I was holding.
I couldn't see the keyhole.
I couldn't see the door.
I couldn't see the house.
I couldn't see Canada.